# SEND HELP

Shirley Mason

Stories

Mason Publishing
Green Valley, AZ
www.shirleymason.com

also by Shirley Mason

Five Couples

The Cav Neumont Saga

The Strength of Water

The Strength of Time

The Strength of Love

The Strength of Mercy

Murder for Short, stories

# Contents

1. Long Distance Marriage      1

2. Elvira Wiggins      11

3. Tandem Yearnings      20

4. Underlining      32

5. Light Gravity      35

6. Saints Be      37

7. Quantum Mercy      50

8. Lately I'm Not Myself      64

9. The Chinese Herb Cure      69

10. The Mannequin      78

11. The Brat      84

12. Bubba's Sidewalk Café      95

13. An Algebra Problem      106

14. C.L.I.K. Man      125

15. Author BIO      140

## Synopsis
Problems with obesity, strange encounters, quantum
events, naturopathic failures, loneliness, spoiled children,
devious mothers-in-law—whatever—the stories in *Send
Help* explore numerous aspects of life in this Universe.

# SEND HELP

Shirley Mason

## A Long Distance Marriage

"I got married during my vacation."

"No!" I don't believe it!"

It was Clive Parker's first day back at work. He had been vacationing for a month in Daytona Beach.

"You're putting us on."

"Not a bit of it. I'm married."

Then they saw the ring: a gold wedding band.

"Bloody Hell!" someone said. "Tell us about her. When will we meet her?"

"I'm not sure about that, guys, she's still down in Florida."

Clive carried his tall, firm 48-year-old form with dignity. His face was easy to look at, and item for item had just the right proportions. His smile was bright and quick. Among the gray was just enough blonde hair left to show that he had been a towhead. He had worked for Steligh Manufacturing for so many years, he knew all of the almost two-thousand employees and was well liked. Sometimes when a pretty, new employee caught his eye, he would give

1

her a special tour of the entire plant. This duty especially pleased him, for with the thin coat of oil covering the floor, without the right shoes, she could easily slide. So any woman getting a tour wearing the wrong shoes, slipping and sliding about so, had to hold on to his arm. When this happened everyone would give him a knowing smile when he passed.

Clive had been divorced since before memory, had lived alone so many years, it was as though he had never been married. No children. All he had to think about was himself and his job as chief plant foreman, which he had done quite well so many years now that he essentially ran the place. He was happy working at Steligh Manufacturing, and had developed many close friends there.

Sometimes he would ask a pretty woman, new to the plant, to join him and his colleagues for lunch in the cafeteria. At lunch he would issue off-color jokes in front of the other men at the table, who would laugh a bit uncomfortably while looking at pretty woman to see whether she looked uncomfortable. So considering the inappropriate jokes, it was not too surprising that Clive had not found someone again to marry. Known only to himself, that was what he wanted in the worst way: to get himself married. During the last year, that need had grown from a faint breeze into an emotional gale.

The plant essentially ran itself without much interference and the same old routine sometimes got to him. He needed a change and for that, he had bought a cottage alongside a stream in New England where he planned to retire. There, he would relax and enjoy peaceful nature. He had been careful to put aside money for an early retirement. His present life wasn't stressful, but he wanted the choice to sleep-in mornings. However, he did not wish to live in his cottage alone; it had come to that. And with his self-confidence supported by good looks and wellbeing, he felt he had a lot to offer a bride of his own, and it troubled him now and then that he had no wife.

This year, that loss had bugged him much more than in years past; that with an entire month's vacation coming up—an entire month to spend somewhere by himself—he had no wife to take with him. For simple and innocent reasons, there wasn't a woman he could, or would, consider asking along.

But he was not downcast about the lonely prospect—no, he had eagerly made plans, bought tickets to Daytona Beach where he would stay in a luxury hotel penthouse overlooking the ocean. Why did he settle on Daytona Beach? No reason really outside of the fact that he had often heard that it was popular with singles of all ages.

All the way down on the flight, he kept thinking wife, wife, wife. He would use this trip to concentrate on finding a wife. She would have to be easy to look at and of course single. And childless; he liked little kids, but over hundreds of lunches, he had listened to his colleagues' stories about problems with children: how complicated they could make life. Other than that, his wife-to-be could be of any religion or race, didn't matter, wasn't important. She could be from Mars; she could be purple. She shouldn't be gay, of course, or—his mind continued to circle the topic—bi. She had to be straight; keep marriage simple. She had to like cats. He had a cat, Willie, boarding in a fancy cattery, who would love to see him when he arrived back at home, vacation over. His wife must like cats.

In Daytona Beach he settled into his fancy penthouse apartment. Nothing but the best, or almost the best. It wasn't actually on the rooftop, but there are two long walls of glass that faced the ocean. He could dive out his window and hit a wave; not something he would be challenged to do, but he could if he had to. He laid his suitcase up on the bed and unpacked, carefully placing all the new shirts and shorts into a bureau drawer, shoes in the closet. He had brought dress shoes, sandals, and sneakers that he wore on the flight. Then he went down to the bar for a beer, and to think about dinner. Always he staked out the women, looked for a wife. This was the trip for a wife. He had waited long enough. Until now he had been too busy or too lazy, he could not decide which, to put forth this major effort. Something had made him wake up; maybe it was the thought of soon moving to the isolated cottage waiting for him.

He took a seat at the side of the bar where he could look over the lounge. His complete attention was given to examining each woman sitting in the crowd. Should he spot a likely candidate for his wife, he would not hesitate a minute to approach her. However, this was proving not to be the easiest decision he had ever made. He had not realized how specific was his wifely requirement. Accompanied by a man, many of the women were obviously on a date. Then there were those in groups such that he could not tell whether they were accompanied. A few were obviously too old—white hair. Then there were a few who look old enough to have white hair; looked old enough, for sure. Wedding bands and diamonds proliferated until he thought they must be handed out at the door. He kept scanning, this took some time in this large room, busy with people. Neither at the bar, nor within the lounge, was there a lone woman. Well, if he wanted to take all the month's vacation, he had plenty of time and plenty of other places to search, including the beach, which he planned to scavenge tomorrow. He was full of hope.

So each morning after he returned up from breakfast—an hour in the restaurant spent scanning the newspaper as well as scanning for any wifely candidates—he slipped into his new Speedo, admired his form in the mirror, tucked into a snug black tee shirt with the words "Wealthy Genius" spread across the front in red block letters, slung over his shoulder a knapsack with his camera and towel and sunscreen, and took the elevator down to the beach.

He staked out a sand spot with his towel and knapsack, and chugged off along the incoming waves. Each day the beach had presented nearly a dozen solitary women for him to approach. And in each case he had stopped to say hello, but had not found the nerve to propose.

Two weeks of his vacation had passed with the exact same results: working the beach and working bars (he tried various) with no wife in hand. And growing restless, he decided he didn't look forward to another similar two weeks. So, on a beautiful, clear and mild, sunny day, he had an epiphany. Something must be done. He must do something radical. He must strike out.

He took the usual beach walk, and ahead he saw several women each of whom looked lovely, and he came to a firm decision: without striking up a conversation to get to know any one of them, he would approach the first one whose looks he admired, and simply ask her to marry him. Just like that!

But when he actually stopped her, he lost some of his nerve. She was really pretty and he had to reassure himself that he' was worthy of her. So he mentally cycled through all the advantages she would have married to him, and he took heart. First, though, he found that he had to engage in some friendly chatter. She seemed interested. She scanned him up and down with a little smile that he thought showed genuine attraction.

Right then, during that first meeting, he actually managed to ask her to marry him. She looked him over with renewed interest, and took her time replying, as she was listening carefully while he sold himself.

Then, "Yes," she said, fully expecting him to cut to the joke.

But he took her hand, said, "You are exactly what I have always dreamed of in a wife. What is your name? My name is Clive Parker."

"I'm Lola," she said, and held tight to his hand. It could be a good thing, she thought, to marry him; he was good looking, and stable: she could tell. And her prospects for a comfortable marriage had been so scant and evasive.

In this manner they walked along the incoming ripples as though they had been engaged for a year. The ripples that washed away the wrinkles of sand, smoothing the surface, seemed to Clive as the incoming of his new life; the smoothing of its wrinkles.

He wasn't impressed with his success, because he knew he was ready and qualified. Had been. He wasn't impressed with his find, because he had for ages imagined the image he wanted and intended to obtain. Success was guaranteed.

Within a few days they married. They were both happy with this decision, and Lola had only one condition to impose on this marriage: she would stay in Daytona Beach, while Clive stayed in Massachusetts to finish out his work years; there were only a few to go. They would act out this marriage on his vacations.

Clive settled for that; and for an understanding that eventually Lola would move up to live with him in his country cottage. He told her all about the lush woods surrounding the cottage, the peace and quiet, the village green not far away, the old-fashioned shops where everyone was welcoming and friendly. How splendid their life there would be. Lola beamed with pleasure as she imagined her future life with Clive.

He was required to work one year longer than he had planned and the next three years passed under their agreed-to circumstances. But that was okay with Lola. She enjoyed his conjugal visits several times during each of those years. Sometimes he could stay with her a month, and other times he came down for long weekends. Money was not a concern, he could buy as many flight tickets as he liked, and when he visited he arrived with gifts, and they would go out shopping to stock Lola up with staples, as well as something pretty. He took her out to eat most nights. They were happy.

Now his retirement day, his last day at work, was here, and the gang—his good colleagues and friends—threw a retirement party for all time. A blast. And they all congratulated him for the future he had talked about for the last three years, that of having his wife join him in retirement in the cottage in the country. On many weekends, Clive had visited the cottage to paint and putty, install new cabinets, finish the hardwood floors, that kind of thing. He had noted that the cottage needed a new roof, and he had planned to get to that soon. He wanted to be there when the new roof went up.

He went to bed and drifted off to sleep in a warm glow. The future he had patiently waited for was upon him. Tomorrow he will fly down to Daytona Beach to help Lola move her things.

She greeted him as usual with love and kisses. She was glad to see him. But she was not ready to move. In fact, she said she loved him, had enjoyed her time with him, but was completely averse to New England, averse to living where it's cold, averse to moving away from Daytona Beach. She said she was so sorry, but to begin with, she hadn't realized how much she thrived in the hot, humid, Florida weather.

Clive was stunned speechless.

She was so sorry, she said again, but she had never realized the seriousness of this plan, and is so sorry that she cannot, will not, move with him. In fact, she'd rather divorce than move.

The peaceful cottage in the country played in Clive's mind; bought years ago and ever since look forward to visiting, monthly, weekly. Resting there. Walking in the woods. Hiking the mountain not so far away. Stopping at the many antique shops. Lounging cold nights before the wonderful, cheerful fireplace. This dream was cemented in place. He had had actual dreams about being there with Lola. He could not live in Daytona Beach. His skin itched every time he arrived there. His teeth ached in Daytona Beach. His feet swelled and tingled. He was allergic to sand, sandflies, excessive humidity, salty air, and congestion of crowds and traffic. He was nervous and anxious away from rural, countrified areas.

At the lodge where the annual Steligh Old Timers' party was held, Clive took a seat, beer in hand, before the giant fireplace. Soon, a group of his old colleagues and friends gathered around to hear how he had been since retirement. He smiled wanly at them, and they noticed a certain quiet new to him. His eyes had grown sad; not at all like him of the past. It was as though he carried a weight, a new weight. As though retirement had placed on him a burden he had not had to carry before. Then the more astute of his friends notice the lack of wedding ring. Why was that? And certain whispers moved among them. But they said nothing to Clive. Spouses don't usually come to the Old Timers' get-togethers, and so it was not surprising that Lola had not come with him.

However, he didn't mind telling his old friends that he was divorced, even though over his last three years at the company, they had had had a blow-by-blow account of his and Lola's happiness. After that it was just hard to get the words out and he had let all opportunities pass.

Finally one of Clive's old friends asked, "How's Lola?"

"She stayed in Daytona. I don't see her anymore."

The old friend grabbed his shoulder and squeezed tight as though to say, "I'm with you buddy."

Clive sat alone now, in the cottage, before the fire. Anyway, he had almost always lived alone. Still his dreams had been moving him forward to companionship. We don't have a guide book, he sometimes thought to himself. He had not had a map to guide him, and so he had struck out blindly. He was not alone actually, for Willie crawled onto his lap.

Outside an unusually heavy snowstorm raged, and as he sat before the fireplace where he had built a blustering fire, Clive continued to hear snow building up on the old creaky roof. A sudden and loud crack worked its way across overhead. Clive quickly rose and carefully, after giving Willie a soft caress, put him down the cellar stairs where the cat had egress should he need it. Then Clive returned and waited before the fire.

# Elvira Wiggins

Elvira Wiggins put on her fur coat, hung her purse over her shoulder, picked up her quilting bag, and car keys, and before she opened the front cut-glass windowed door, she stopped a second to check her lipstick in the small, ornate mirror that hung adjacent to the door. She adjusted her wig. It was the wig with slightly red touches, and she thought it was fine enough that no one knew the wig-nature of it; her hair was growing so thin.

She was on her way to the neighborhood sewing-bee, and with great pride, for the quilt that had taken a year for her to make, had recently won the blue ribbon at the annual state fair. Her fingertips were all pricked from the tiny stitches on lace that wandered about adorning the fabric in an irregular manner.

Janet had made fun of it; lace woven over a quilt! she had laughed. She would. Well, she's not laughing now, Elvira smiled to herself, remembering.

For the past two years, Janet's wall hangings had taken that blue ribbon, and up until now she thought she was the Queen Bee. Most of the club's members worked only on small stuff: aprons, napkins, those kinds of things. Only Elvira and Mary and Bonny tackled time-consuming quilts. Today, Elvira was looking forward to witnessing Janet's mood, for she had actually taken no prize this year at the fair; unusual for Janet. Elvira thought it might even be possible that Janet wouldn't show up at today's sewing bee.

The workshop was at Mary's house, and although that was but four blocks away, an easy stroll for Elvira, she would enjoy displaying her new Lexus. She pictured slowly pulling the car up to the curb in easy view of the house. She would take her time putting the car into park, releasing the seat belt, and gathering her purse and quilting bag. Some of the gals might still be in the front room by the large picture window, and she would allow time for them to see for certain that this was her car. None of the gals had a car to quite match it; even their Cadillacs were two years old now. If they teased her about driving instead of walking, she would just say she felt a bit tired today for carrying everything.

That made sense, for she was pretty far along with her quilt of yellow and blue—primary colors with a large star burst—it had become bulky and heavy. These days she felt like a star, what with winning the blue ribbon at the state fair, the biggest prize of all, and now arriving in this shiny new Lexus. It had been tough hearing about Janet's trips around the world every two years, while Raymond never took her anywhere; always said he couldn't take the time off, certainly wouldn't go anywhere where English wasn't the native language. And if Elvira would mention to him that she hoped to see Paris or Rome, he would always reply, "You're crazy," though, he did say it gently.

12

All-in-all, he and she did get along quite well. She had the best husband, she thought. And she had not let time cause her to drop her usual welcome for him—started when they first married—when in the evenings he came into the kitchen, she had always, with a bright smile, said to him, "Sweetie-heart-love is home. Life begins when sweetie-heart-love is home." She always thought that he seemed to appreciate her greeting. Surely now, if they saw the Lexus, the gals would feel a touch of envy and think that she did indeed have the best husband. After all those years hearing about their trips, after which they would inevitably ask her where she had been, followed by her inevitable answer, said with an assuring, though forced smile:

"Raymond's business just won't allow him to leave . . . he's in such demand. But he's talking about selling his company . . . then we can take off."

And Elvira's chin, brow, and shoulders would invariably lift an inch or so with assurance.

But that excuse had grown old and solicited smiling, patronizing nods. Still, she couldn't imagine anyone else's husband coming home with a new Lexus, nor any new car, for that matter. For a minute, she mused that the Lexus was in Raymond's name; that was okay, she knew his intention was that it was her own, not his. She further mused that, actually, it wasn't like Raymond either, to buy an expensive car, just like that. Two days ago he had left the house in her old Ford and returned in the Lexus, all smiles. True, it was near her birthday, but still . . . . Too bad he hadn't bought the car before she made that long two-day drive to visit her daughter in Omaha.

Now her thoughts turned to Janet, with her bold thighs always on display in her short, too short, skirt. Nearly up to her butt. Didn't believe rational men liked that sort of display, certainly not on their own wives. Raymond wouldn't, she thought, not in this small town where everyone knew everyone. He was too conservative—had a high sense of dignity; though perhaps in her own case, though he didn't say so, there was too much thigh to display. Well, this year, the ribbon was hers—and would be again she imagined; the Lexus was hers, and the generous husband was hers.

She had poked along so mesmerized by these thoughts, that when she pulled along the curb across from Mary's house, she saw several of the cars belonging to clubwomen. As she had planned, she took her time parking, settling the car, removing her seatbelt, and gathering her purse and quilting bag. She wouldn't look to see whether anyone was watching from Mary's large front window to witness her emerging from this splendid, glossy steed. She would be so casual, thinking nothing unusual—still, she held her head a bit higher, and formed a satisfied, smug little smile.

As she headed up Mary's walk, she continued to avoid checking the window, although she thought she could feel stares. She expected that they had been waiting for her arrival to start the tea. Rest assured: the article about her quilt, its photograph in the local paper, and the Lexus—she was taking all this in stride. Just normal everyday stuff. Yet, entering the door, always unlocked for these meetings, her heart fluttered a second, her resolve shifted slightly as she saw everyone already working around the dining room table, and enjoying their tea.

While receiving their stares and hellos, she worked her face: whether to smile back knowingly, or pretend she had nothing in mind except where to put her first stitches this day. She took her seat and looked around expecting smiles and congratulations, but all seemed intent on their competent stitches.

Finally Mary said, "Oh, let's all congratulate Elvira on her blue ribbon. She's been due for some good luck."

As she said this, Elvira noticed the slightly sticky smile, that Janet forced. But the others, Mary and Bonny, looked up and did say the appropriate words. Elvira wondered about the amused look Janet was sending her; almost as if she knew something unusual, not at all about the blue ribbon. Well, Janet would learn. Had they seen the Lexus? They were strangely silent as their needles poked in and out.

She threaded a needle and began a stitch. Thinking about the car had turned her thoughts again to Raymond; he had seemed happier lately, more thoughtful to her, had even begun standing around the kitchen, martini in hand, whilst she sautéed something for their dinner. And he would respond to her conversation with appropriate and cheerful replies; whereas before he could be expected to park himself before the TV, and in answer to anything she called to him, would merely grunt.

Soon, the women's topic turned to sex. Bonny said she had just seen an ad for a movie where "they were really doing it." Amid snickers, eyes rolled.

"Tell me! Tell me the name!" said Mary, her face pushing up into an eager grin.

"Mary," Bonny said, "you mean you are not getting enough? With that sexy looking husband of yours, I would think you'd be even weary of sex."

"Sexy looking aside, he is usually too tired. His age is creeping up. We haven't had a good romp in a while, and I don't think one is soon on our timeline."

"I know just what you mean," Bonny said, "S'why I mentioned the movie. Something I've been missing these days as well. Seems when our guys reach fifty, they've had all of us they wanted."

15

"Really, Bonny, that's putting it crudely," said Mary.

"Well, I'm just saying." Bonny's face looked a touch sad as she looked down to perfect a stitch.

"Janet, you look rather smug," Mary poked. "I'd think with your husband gone so much, you'd have complaints of your own."

Janet simply smiled, wagged her head as though to say, "No comment," and appeared to concentrate on the fabric before her.

"Hrump, Janet! You are sometimes an enigma for the rest of us."

Janet's smile grew broader, but still she had no comment.

"Girls . . . I think somehow, Janet is getting satisfied," said Mary.

A round of snickers circled the table, and for the rest of this quilting-bee, nothing more was said about sex, the abundance of it, or the lack.

The day had come for the meeting to be held at Elvira Wiggin's house, and whereas a few weeks before she would have left the Lexus out by the curb, now it was carefully stowed in the garage. The blue ribbon, however, largely forgotten by the group, was proudly displayed on Elvira's living room mantle, as a silent reminder. And this day no one brought up the topic of sex; it had run its course; although they did still notice that Janet seemed more content than the rest of them. What was on Janet's mind, Elvira wondered—thought she seemed to keep studying her. Janet would look over at Elvira, then look down to work a stitch, then look back up at Elvira, always with that slightly smug smile.

The quilts, in different stages of completion, were growing; more and more developing their soft and lovely patterns. Around Elvira's extra-large dining room table, the ladies could spread out and work faster. Much was accomplished this day and each seemed pleased. Especially Janet.

After Elvira served tea and cakes they packed their bundles, said their goodbyes and thank-you's and left—all but Janet, that is. She hung back, then took a seat in the living room. "I just want to sit a bit," she said as Elvira looked at her with a question. "I've gotten so much done today that I want to gather my energy before I head on home."

"Of course." Elvira was puzzled; this was not at all like Janet. She had indeed been slightly strange lately. She looked to be working on an obsession; something on her mind; something out of place, something not pleasant. And Janet's gaze was fixed on the blue ribbon. "May I offer you another cup of tea?" Elvira said.

"No dear. I am thinking about an important matter that perhaps you should know."

"Oh?" To receive whatever Janet had to say, couldn't be beneficial based on Janet's warning look. Elvira sat down on the upholstered in rare-French-paisley Queen Ann wingback chair she had always loved so much, and from which she always drew comfort. She faced Janet across the room.

Janet pulled her attention away from the ribbon and focused on Elvira. "Your husband and I are having sex right in this very house, sometimes in your own bed," she said, nodding her head affirmatively.

At first, amid her struggle to find that Janet was trying for a very poor joke, Elvira couldn't hear her words. She turned her glance away from Janet, but she saw, by the woman's image in a mirror hanging to the side, that Janet was dead serious. Slowly the words began to have meaning. She looked around as though she might find a spot of information with which to organize and assimilate Janet's smug announcement. What was Janet's intent? Then, hoping to find the explanation, she looked up at her to explain this outrage.

There was a long pause in the room while the two women studied each other.

Janet seemed overly secure.

When Elvira said nothing, still searching for meaning in this bazar, unbelievable confession, Janet raised her head in a pose, chin up, and said, "You've become so self-important with your Lexus and your blue ribbon that I just thought you should know. We haven't even taken a motel room. We just go at it big time. Right here. And laugh about your wig. Especially when you were visiting your daughter—the days were not long enough for us."

There was another long, still, pause in the room.

The ticking of a tiny gold clock on the table next to Elvira reminded her of the day Raymond had given it to her. Pure gold. He must have loved her so much to think of her when he saw this beautiful thing.

"I'm tired of Raymond now," Janet said. "I could have had him, but he's yours if you still want him. Just thought you should know."

With this last speech, Janet had stood, wrapped her coat around her, picked up her sewing bag and purse, and without so much as a nod back to distraught and dumb-struck Elvira, she let herself out the front door.

Elvira sat. She looked into the mirror at the place where Janet had been sitting, and Janet's ghost seemed to be relaxing on the couch, smiling back at her. Oddly, her only thought was about the comfort she had always felt in her Queen Ann, upholstered in rare-French-paisley, wingback chair. That was the unique thought in place of which she could not swap a rational idea. Right now the chair was cold, though she tried to imagine a future time when again it would seem cozy. She could not. Would it ever feel wonderful again? Raymond. That bastard. What had she missed? Now she knew why he had bought the Lexus. Well, he could have the damn car. And Janet. She wanted no more of either of them. She would kiss off both of them and drop out of the sewing bee; not have to see Janet's face ever again. Nor Raymond's for that matter, if she could arrange it. When he had seemed most happy with her and with his home, she mused, he must instead have been pleased with his memory of exploring Janet's short skirt, and her bold thighs.

The day began to pull in its light, but Elvira stayed, slouching lower in the chair. Dinner. There would be no dinner tonight, or perhaps it would be something pulled from the freezer to microwave. How could she explain this to Raymond? He knew she thrived on cooking good dinners. For new ideas, her favorite cookbook was always open on the kitchen table.

The sounds of his car in the drive and the garage door lifting broke her reverie. He would be in soon. Later she would pack her bags and leave. Then she remembered that the Lexus was not in her name. She must arrange a smile and a reason why dinner was not cooked.

"Hello, dear," she offered with a tight, forced smile, her words tripling upward unnaturally. "Sweetie-heart-love is home. Life begins when sweetie-heart-love is home."

# Tandem Yearnings

**M**y wife, Joanna, and I could hardly wait to hit the road on one of our tandem twenty-four-speed bicycles. That day, a bright, clear Saturday morning, we chose the white Cannondale, as we would be wearing our matching sets with psychedelic red-white-and-blue zigzags. Joanna cut a lean, lyrical figure, and I flattered myself that my masculine form matched her feminine one. It was the Fourth of July weekend, and we were ready to put on our show.

We rode as one, legs perfectly inching forward and down, inching back and up, unleashing our impeccable machine. Around the town of Green Valley, Joanna and I had come to be known as a dazzling movement of four legs on two wheels.

Green Valley, with biking paths through most of the town, was a good choice for cyclers. And taking pride in our reputation, we had bought three valuable tandem bicycles; one specially made for us by Cannondale. And in time we owned a dozen cycling outfits. Matching. Hers and mine. We melded with the bikes into one flowing colorful unit; graceful and moving with the coordination of a symphony. When we peddled gently, I could hear *That Sheep May Safely Graze* resounding in my head, and when we pushed aggressively, the *Song of the Volga Boatmen* seemed to surge with each stroke: *Yo-o heave ho!*

Both Joanna and I had careers that left our weekends free, and we usually managed to complete long rides on both Saturday and Sunday. Some of the regulars along our paths purposely watched for us. After riding, we would toss out suits in for a quick wash, and while Joanna hung them on the clothesline, I would pour wine for us, and we would relax in the back garden facing the desert. Then often, with my Glock 23, I would take pot shots at the line of colorful patches of prayer flags that Joanna had hung after artfully cutting them from our discarded, faded suits. We liked to imagine that each time I hit a prayer flag, a prayer went up.

Tandem prayers.

I say, we *usually* managed to ride, as we had one impediment: my father.

Pops lived in Green Valley. Joanna and I had moved here from Tucson to have a bit of family and give him some assistance. He was now closer to eighty than seventy, and though he had a high-performance body, he was unsteady, and, as well, he needed our company.

Our first years living in Green Valley went uneventfully. I taught medieval history at Arizona State, and Joanna, a scientist, worked in a lab testing blood samples for illegal drugs. Weekend mornings were for our rides, which left afternoons and evenings free to help Pops shop, or join him for a meal. He liked to go out for pizza; although as time went by, that became something of a problem for Joanna and me, because Pops ordered pizza more and more frequently, and Joanna and I had to watch our weight in order to fit into our streamlined biking outfits. We didn't intend to stop cutting a figure, you might say. Biking was certainly our first love, and Pops, an ornery old bastard didn't give a damn. Joanna and I humored him. After all, our thinking at the time was, how much longer would he be alive? Therefore we would order a small pizza for Pops and a salad for Joanna and me. Soon, however salads became boring but we only ate with Pops about one night a week, so we managed.

We thought life would continue in this peaceful manner, perhaps another decade, so Joanna and I ordered additional vibrant biking outfits until we had all the color combinations possible. In order to display our costumes carefully, and find each with ease, we had a special closet built in which we arranged the sets much like in a retail store: matching helmets on a top hook, tops and bottoms in the middle, high tech shoes on a rack below. We had only to look across the array of stripes, angles, and swirls to yearn to be out on a tandem.

One day Joanna woke up not feeling well. Most unusual for her.

"Just a sharp headache," she said. "Hon, would you please bring me an ice pack?"

I quickly complied.

"What do you think gave you a headache?" I asked, handing the pack to her; I had carefully wrapped it with a soft cotton napkin to ease the icy shock.

"Perhaps I read too long last night."

That was plausible; it was our custom to read before going to sleep. I tried to repel negative thoughts; still I went to work that day feeling a kink in things, and yearning for normalcy. Joanna had a headache strong enough to keep her in bed! Not like her at all. What is normal? I guessed there was no such thing, and any assumption otherwise was an illusion.

During the day, I called Joanna to see whether her headache had eased, but there was no answer. She was probably sleeping and had turned off the phone. When I reached home, I entered the house calling for Joanna. No answer. I went into the bedroom, and there she was, still in bed. Not moving.

"Joanna!" I yelled. I shook her. She didn't respond. I felt for a pulse. There was none. Joanna, my life, my tandem bicycling partner, almost my twin, died. Dead. Joanna was dead.

First I had to call 911, and then I ordered an autopsy. I hated to ravage Joanna's body, but I needed to know what had happened to my beloved partner.

Next I had to tell Pops.

"Just prop her up on a bicycle," Pops said, when I finally got him on the phone.

"Pops, she died!"

"Well, just prop her up on a bicycle. She'll pull through."

"Pops!"

"It's nothing I did here," he said. "I had nothing to do with it."

What was Pops thinking? He didn't sound like himself. Well, I couldn't worry about him now. I'd find out more later.

The next week struck me with alternating fits of disbelief and spasms of sadness. I zombie-walked through the days.

The autopsy revealed that Joanna had had a massive brain aneurism. She had never had a chance. Poor thing. Poor me. Somehow I reeled through the funeral like a man on a tandem bike with a drunken partner, struggling to keep control. If I could have, I would have given Joanna a granite bicycle for her gravestone. Or I would have had a mausoleum erected and placed her favorite bike (the yellow one on which we rode in our yellow-white-and-gray suits) inside with her. However, with my more modest circumstances I could only bury her in the biking outfit in which she looked her best. That became a tough decision, because, in all our dozen and more outfits, she had been a stellar vision.

I finally decided on the set covered with psychedelic flames: orange-red-and-white flames on black. I had a moment's pause to convince myself that that had nothing to do with burning in Hell. Such a sweet innocent as she was, I assured myself, our Great Bicyclist up there would see to it that she went the right way. I folded carefully and placed in with her, my matching flames outfit. I would not be wearing that again, and perhaps her soul could derive some comfort from its presence.

What would I do now?

I had to go to work. I couldn't neglect my students, and the substitute professor was way behind the class; completely unfamiliar with medieval history. I doubted that he had even heard of the Carolingian Empire. I began to have the peace needed to teach my classes and deal with Joanna's belongings. All those beautiful biking outfits. Two of each. Hers and mine.

As I began to pack away Joanna's, I felt the full impact of my double loss: my mate and my tandem partner, the one who matched me. Not many couples (maybe none) could say they blended so well. I looked at each beautiful outfit as I folded it into a trunk. There was the fuchsia-with-green-swirls and green-and-fuchsia sleeve and thigh cuffs. Stunning.

We had been a sight in our fuchsia sets with those fuchsia stripes bending and straightening down our legs. Then I packed the red-white-and-blue that we had been amused to wear on the Fourth. Bystanders actually clapped.

This was too painful. I had to stop for a while, and I poured myself a marching martini and sat, feet propped up, threading my inner vision through the cycling closet. I could picture all those sets. What a waste. It would never work for me to buy a single-rider bike and wear my getup without Joanna. On the tandem, she and I had been as synergistic as a ballet duo.

Through these horrific events all my cycling stopped. Anyway I couldn't ride a tandem bike alone.

More sullen and somber weeks went by and then one day on my drive to work it came to me that more than most, I needed a suitable companion. She would have to be a certain size and age. Have to be slender. Must be strong and leggy. Must like to ride a bicycle. I could try to fill in Joanna's place; that wouldn't be the same as replacing Joanna.

I signed on to Match.com and was extremely specific about my requirements. Within two days I had enough replies to start interviewing. I wanted my applicants to come right to my house, and I assured them that I sought a long-term relationship, and wished to show them where we would live. (Staying put was essential; Green Valley was too good a riding local for me to move away.) Then I waited for the first woman to arrive.

People are not honest with themselves. Why would a five-foot-four, hundred-and-fifty-pound girl of eighteen reply to an ad that specifically said five-feet-six, one-twenty pounds, age thirty to forty? We had swapped pictures, talked on the phone, but she had lied, lied, lied. A waste of my time.

The next woman didn't show and I never heard from her again. I saw I had a dating-site learning curve to traverse. I did more thorough due diligence and the third woman, Nina, had possibilities. First I offered her a glass of wine, which she accepted, then I went for the trunk and explained, as I pulled out a particularly striking outfit, light-gray-with-one-red-shoulder and knickers with one red leg, what she was to do: go into the guest room and put it on. Naturally I said please.

"Whose clothes are these?" she asked first.

"My deceased wife's."

"And you want me to wear them?"

"Indeed. You look like they'll fit you perfectly."

But, she tossed into the trunk the lovely, and expensive, I might add, gray-with-red. Turning to me, she tightened her eyes, and gave me a sneer. "Not on your life. Not on your wife's death."

I thought the windows would shatter as the slam she gave the door on her sudden way out, vibrated through the house. You didn't have to get your knickers in a knot, I thought.

It was Sunday and I couldn't retrieve an upbeat feeling. I called Pops to go for pizza, and he said yes. But going through the garage I could hear the ssssshhh, ssssshhh, ssssshhh of tires wanting to run the paths; I felt the bikes had heads which they turned to me—imploring. I could see on each an image of Joanna and me, pumping, pushing with completely coordinated colors and moves. One tire started to turn and Joanna seemed to call to me. I had to get out of there fast. I hurried to pick up Pops.

He said he was doing okay, but hoped we could get together more frequently. In my heart I wished him well, but at that time I had problems of my own, including emotional, that needed attention.

"I'm looking for a riding companion," I said to Pops. I didn't go into my hoping she would be more than just someone with whom to ride. "I have three valuable tandem bicycles, I'm sure you know, and I want to utilize them. They're such a pleasure to ride, so, as I said, I'm working on finding a riding partner. Even so, I'll try to make more time to take you about."

"Bring her with you."

In my Match.com blurb I didn't want to be too specific; as say, wear dead wife's clothing and go tandem bike riding with me. Guess I was just going to have to get lucky, and I continued to interview.

Soon I had a long talk with a new Match.com find, Mavis. In our phone conversations, I had asked her to send me her most recent photo, and her most recent weight. She sounded pleasant; laughed a lot; said she regularly rode a bike. She came for an interview.

After we had laughed over a glass of wine while I explained my situation and showed her the bikes, I brought out the trunk. But I had been surreptitiously trying to size her up. Not easy to do. I suspected she was too hippy—and sure enough, when she tried on that slinky blue-with-white-wings across the clavicle as well as across the bun, her hips were wide and pivotal. I shuddered at the thought of wings waving at passersby as they had a look at her bun. I hated to tell her. And couldn't.

"I'll get back to you. It's been lovely."

I interviewed three more women, but they didn't fit. We tried two of my favorites: the black-with-shocking-day-glow bars scattered randomly across the top, and the gold-and-blue divided diagonally down the high-tech latex shirt with matching cuffs.

We also tried another—I've forgotten now which, but in each case something didn't fit, didn't look right. I would walk passed my tandems and tell them not to give up hope, but my own hopes were faltering.

Then came Lila. Everything about Lila seemed perfect. I leveled with her right off and she accepted the situation. An intelligent and caring woman, she worked as therapist for the handicapped, and the bonus was that she fit perfectly into each of Joanna's outfits. She was lean and lithesome. I was delighted, as was she.

First, I had asked her to wear the black-and-white striped set. This set, when moving, created an optical illusion. Observers loved the affect; almost made them dizzy. Lila and I spent a day trying on the sets; I served her a fine lunch and we laughed a lot. She ooh'd and aah'd over each pair and wanted to see how I looked in several. Then we rode. Riding with Lila I could feel her slight unsteadiness, but the next day, in the royal blue-with-day-glow-lime swirls, Lila was steady as a ropewalker. It felt wonderful to have her behind me on the tandem.

That evening I explained that I had to take Pops for pizza.

"I'd love to go with you," Lila said. "I love pizza, and I want to meet the gentleman who turned out such a fine, handsome son."

I must have beamed—the idea that I had found a co-rider who would also join me with Pops. For two months that's how it went. Lila blended right in with the bikes, the apparel, Pops, pizza and me. In another month Lila moved in.

But then, after another month, things, silently stepping down one slinky-step at a time, began to change. At first it was an innocent withdrawal of Lila's.

"I want to stay in tonight," she said one Sunday. "You go ahead and have a nice time with Pops."

I didn't see this as the rebellion it was to become, until the following Sunday, Lila again took a stand.

"I think you and I should have a quiet dinner together tonight," she said.

I didn't mind; sounded reasonable. We were overdue. We had probably been riding too much due to my excitement getting back on wheels. But Pops didn't like it—the second Sunday in a row—he looked forward to our meals together. I could almost see his scowl through the phone.

"Sorry, Pops, I guarantee we won't miss next week."

But we did.

Lila said she had a persistent headache, and of course, in view of what had happened to Joanna, I was afraid to leave her alone. Then Pops took a bad turn: at dusk one evening, on the way to his car, he tripped over a curb and sprained his ankle. He was now housebound and reduced to using crutches. He hired a part-time caregiver to clean and do laundry, but I felt anxious that he had at least one good meal a day. I approached Lila about this.

"It's temporary, Lila. He's eager to be independent again. Nothing serious happened and once the swelling subsides, he'll be driving again."

"Pops is too demanding," she said. "We might as well be living with him. I'm here for you, not Pops. I help handicapped all week. I get my fill."

"Lila, it's just for dinner. We'll go over about 5:00, have our cocktail with him, watch the Santa Ritas turn pink while I grill and you cook rice. I'll make a salad to take with us."

Lila accompanied me to Pops' for two of those dinners. However, the next Sunday she said she had had too challenging a workweek and wouldn't be

riding, or going out. I had been looking forward to
our wearing the solid-black tri suit, orchid sides, mid-
thigh leg-length with orchid cuffs. Thought about that
at work even, between classes. Her dropping out was
quite a setback for me, but I said nothing; Pops was
looking forward to his dinner. I made a salad, I had
already bought steaks to take, and I left.

When I got home, all Lila's things were gone.
She had packed up and left a note.

"You're a lovely man, but it turns out I don't
enjoy all this cycling, and having to share our lives."

I was not too surprised. I guess I had sensed her
discontent more than I wanted to admit. Even so, I
sank into a torpor; I felt that I had lost Joanna two
times over. I wandered around the house trying to
focus on what was a true problem versus what was
not. I made a slothful martini, not usual for me after
dinner; put on *Le Sacre du Printemps*—that always
gets me going—and set about wiping down the
platinum-and-turquoise tandem. The exquisite
workmanship and beauty of these machines generally
soothed my soul.

But what to do next?

I thought about tandem cycling—a masterpiece of
art moving along in those vibrant, even dazzling,
outfits. I thought about the effort of looking for
another riding partner. The precision of the
requirements: ability, inclination, fit, willingness to
help Pops. And the future seemed formidable.

I pictured Joanna and me returning from a ride
and tossing the suits into the wash; sponging down
shoes and helmet, and hanging them for five minutes
on the back clothesline. Thinking about this, I knew
what to do. It took half-an-hour to gather all the
outfits, both hers and mine, and to hang all pieces on
the line. Then I put on the *1812 Overture*, freshened

my martini, carried it and my Glock 23 outside, and sat facing the clothesline.

I said, "Thank you. Goodbye . . . Goodbye . . . Goodbye."

The 1812 cannons seemed to explode with each pop. It was particularly challenging to hit certain thin stripes. The helmets were especially rewarding as they split with loud satisfying cracks. I enjoyed making the shoes spin, and hearing the thud sound that I could hear even over the knelling of the 1812 carillon. When shreds of orange, green, purple, fuchsia, yellow, black, white, red and blue curled and twisted in the breeze, I pictured the bikes and wondered how hard it would be to cut through their carbon frames.

# Underlining

On certain days you forget why you're here. You
know how it is. You have a job to do and you
want to stay with it, stay focused, but you wake with
muddled thinking, and for a while can't remember
what it is you have to do. *They* try to distract you.
Idiots. (Just saying.) It's a prick on their perfect
selves that they can't do the job as well as you. Been
there before? Then you know what it's like; genius is
under appreciated. On those days, and today is one of
those days, it takes a lot of effort to sit up, let alone
move your arm and get your fingers moving. You try
to think why you're here. You look around, and
wonder why the walls are covered with lines. Some
on the floor. Long lines, short lines, wavy lines. Then
you see the pens, and your thoughts move into focus;
you connect pens with lines. Now you remember why
you're here. (Really, some days are like this.) You're
here to finish underlining for *them*, for in all their
perfection, they've been unable to do the job as well
as you. Each tiny pinprick of imperfection on the

walls must be underlined. You look for the spot where you left off before they carried you out of the room. Ah, you've finished two walls. Two to go. You look at the ceiling and hope they realize you need a ladder if they expect you to underline there. You rouse, pick up the pen (thank you, *they've* provided a box full of pens, but only after you demonstrated in ways you'd rather forget), and head on over to wall three, where only a dozen or so lines are in place.

Now you remember that when you drew that last line you ran into the hole; a tiny imperfection and you flew into a rage when you couldn't properly underline that spot. That was when they carried you off. What did they expect? If they don't want the job done perfectly, get someone else! Well, that hole doesn't look so important now. So you start underlining next to the hole. You think that you must have been underlining for them for months now, and you haven't yet had a paycheck.

Sometimes you ask yourself, how did you get so proficient at underlining? You think back. Way back. It started with your books by Anita Brookner and Brian Greene. Both using words you had to learn. Too many at times. You couldn't have managed without a good pen and lots of underlining; ink a line under this esoteric word; another under that baffling word. Each had represented something you didn't know, would have to look up, or wanted to remember. A word or two per page usually. And back in those days your underlining was weak; truly, it's a skill to develop.

You continue. But what a tosser this pen is. How do they expect you to draw quality lines with this pen? Some lines need to be fragile as a wren's leg; some need to be bold as a crow's. They'll just have to be content with the outcome; you're stuck with the pens at hand. No idea how long it'll take them to return. Sometimes you don't see them for days during which they slide meals through the slot. Underline. Eat. Underline. Eat. That can be hard; it gets kind of messy, but you're up for it; your skills are perfect now. You underline a pea; then eat it. And so on. When you finish, the plate is perfectly lined. They appreciate that.

Many imperfections and perfections on this wall; both need an underline. You think sometimes maybe you'll never finish. As you continue across the wall, you remember again how your underlining skills grew. The day came when you knew that many more words, phrases, sentences, and paragraphs needed marking. Nothing was unimportant. Nothing. Soon, with all your books underlined, you looked around and understood that books were insignificant compared to life at large. Life: the furnishings of life. The couch, the lamp, coffee table, chair, the cat, toothpaste—all were significant and required underlining. You went out for boxes of pens, and courageously began the task. But why was Jeannette so upset when she visited and saw all the lines? Then you realized that she had to bring you to this place for *they* desperately needed your work. And the meals are good, and you don't have to stop what you're doing to cook or wash dishes. Not to brag, but you know how it is.

# Light Gravity

Whipping my Cannondale bicycle up for a wheelie and into my science teacher, knocking her down, I watch her car keys slip from her grasp. She looked stunned as we both watched the keys fly upward. We had just stepped into a universe with lighter gravity to which we were not normally conditioned. The keys stayed in place about fifteen feet aloft, and I realized that, as well, I felt a bit lighter. Fortunately, my science teacher could not see me, because of a trick I had figured out while meddling with photons, whereby I could make them bypass me, I was invisible. This witty and wise woman did not know what had hit her.

This was a good thing, for I was already on her bad side for telling her that neutrinos had punched 6 billion holes in my homework. She didn't believe this; she had fallen for the myth that neutrinos rarely interacted with matter. But honest it was true; at least I imagined it to be true, and that which one can imagine, can be true.

While she waited, straining her neck skyward, hoping her keys would drift down (they weren't about to, as far as I could tell), I squeezed into a sidewise universe and stepped into the grocery store on my right. I relaxed my photon trick so the grocery clerk could see me, and I did the honest thing—paid for a Snickers candy bar.

Well, it was honest for the moment anyway, for as soon as I slipped back into my home universe, the dollar I had spent, would disappear from the grocer's drawer and arrive back in my hand; a simple example of tunneling. And still I got to eat the Snickers.

I thought I would wait around to see how Teach managed without keys, when I remembered that I could gather some Higgs Bosons and with them ignite her car's engine. Ignite, meaning get the ignition going. So I did that. Teach stared at the car —its engine running. It took her five seconds to decide to use the car and get out of there. It had started to levitate, due to the weaker gravity and she didn't want to lose it.

Too bad I can't brag about starting the car. But she would never believe I was there. It will be fun to hear whether she ever retrieved her keys, and to hear her version of how she got the car started.

# Saints Be

The reason I couldn't see the Tiger Rattlesnake
that struck my ankle was because the fat that
hung out over my front excluded any view of my
feet, or anything below my navel. So I spent a week
in hospital with a swollen leg that was nearly ready to
be removed (as in amputated). As tragic as that was
in and of itself, it would mean an end to my career as
a fat model (model as in high fashion for the
oversized set, and fat as in obese, and obese as in
wallowing in the after effects of years consuming
bread bacon butter chips cheese cakes pasta pizza
French fries and ice-cream—lots of it). How did I
become a model with so much excess baggage? The
answer is my face, skin and hair are perfect (as in
angelic), and my feet are tiny and flawless. Despite
the bulk, I am considered beautiful. When women
who are overweight see ads for "Rubenesque"
fashions, they can imagine their own beauty. I was
well paid. I was the fatnip for fat fashionistas.

With only one leg, I would disqualify instantly,
for even though I could never stand for long, I do

often have to stand for the photographer. When I endure a modeling session, I have to go through several changes of clothing, yes several—bikinis, workout or jogging apparel, gowns and what all. Crowds gathered to watch this unusual phenomenon; few had opportunities to witness such pulchritude. Be clear, though, I had always resisted nude modeling for obvious reason. My point is, there was money in bulk.

So I, living part of the year in a rattle-snaky area, thought I at least ought to slim down enough so I could see snakes when they ventured to my doorway. I was thinking this as I lay in bed, leg raised, anti-venom injected, antibiotic saturated, in pain pretty much. Being in hospital got me off to a good start, for I had no access to all the ice-cream I had become addicted to over the years to say nothing about BLT's cheeseburgers French fries and pizza.

Thus it happened that during my week of hospitalization, I lost twenty pounds, more than three per day. I was on my way. I had to be careful though, not to lose more than would lose my job. My agency had a waiting list of photo ops for me, and a show lined up for fashion week. We fatties drew a huge crowd as we walked the runway, and our agents didn't want to lose that income. Sometimes during those shows, they would ask us to jog, or run, but we would complain that it was hard on our ankles. Sometimes we did try. The crowd loved it. I spent a moment's reflection on whether they wanted to see the designs, or the huge models wiggling along, one hip in each hemisphere. Twenty pounds made no difference to my photographers, so once released from the hospital and on my feet—although, I still had to ice my injured ankle every hour or so—the modeling assignments continued and money poured in. My ankle was still swollen, but it hardly showed, subsumed amid other fat deposits.

The first thing a single person (single as in lives alone) immediately thinks of when leaving a hospital, is food. Lots of it—cheeseburgers BLT's and ice-cream. Ice-cream topped the list, and my first stop was the grocery store. I also wanted to load up on potatoes sour cream for potatoes frozen French fries chips bacon bread and butter. Succulent aromas of melted cheese and grilled beef dripping with fat dwelled in my olfactories. As I drove, I thought about the snake—my ankle still throbbed a bit—and about my thought to lose enough to see over my belly. Well, one day—for rewarding myself for the ordeal I had just been through, including loss of a bit of income—to eat exactly as I desired without thought of calories, couldn't make a difference. I would start watching my intake tomorrow.

And I did just that. The next day, instead of having two bacon-cheeseburgers and two sodas, French fries and one pint of ice cream three times a day, I had one bacon-cheeseburger, one soda, one pint of ice cream. I put on the *Holbein Suite* quite loudly so as not to hear the rumblings emanating from my belly. Big belly, big rumblings, big emanations. Soon, I found that I had more spare money, for I was buying only three pounds of cheese, and two pounds of butter, and four pounds of ground beef per week, quite a reduction in bulk and money.

On a day off, I took myself on a shopping spree, and although it was still hard to find my size, I bought slacks. This was something, as I usually bought online at sites for the oversized. (My crowd thrilled when retail came online so we could buy in the privacy of our own homes.) Sometimes I am allowed to buy fashions I have worn in shows or photo-ops, so I am always dressed in style: delicate drapings, gossamer scarves, and such.

After three weeks of this reduced diet, I fit just a tiny bit easier in my first class seat to NY, and in my boyfriend's car. Speaking of car, both he and I had always wanted a sports car, but neither of us would have fit into one. Yes, he was about my size, and he loved me for my size. With me, he didn't feel so gargantuan. His name is Terry, and he has his own company. He had had to start it because of prejudice in hiring. It's turned out to be enormously good luck for he's worth his weight in gold now, and that's a lot. Terry noticed my new slacks, but not the loss of another twenty pounds. Considering my size, twenty pounds were a drop in the black hole of bulk.

I still couldn't see a rattlesnake at my feet, and when my ankle ached, visions crept in of the hospital and its scant meals. And, living part of the year in Green Valley with desert all around, I was always in threat of another episode with a rattler. Maybe a few more pounds would solve the problem. After all, I didn't want to lose too much. Didn't want to lose my job—the assignments were rolling in. It took some hard, hunger-making-thinking to think this through. Less food consumption was in order. Painful as it was to contemplate, I had to further reduce my intake. You may ask, did I count calories? and the answer is no. I was never good at counting.

I should have said straight off that I had to weigh at the gym, because an ordinary household scale didn't approach my weight. I would go to the gym at 7:00 P.M. when often no one was there so I could weigh in the privacy of my own bulk. Did I ever exercise? you might well ask, and the answer is no. I had to protect my income, and as well, I had a hard enough time moving around the house, let alone walking down the street.

Thinking it over while riding around with Terry, I decided that maybe, just maybe I could drop one of the daily pints of ice cream. No, that was the item I most craved. Probably I could do without French fries. I pictured fries dipped in mustard, and I drooled. But I stopped buying French fries. Even that allowed for more cash at the month's end, and my bank account grew. What would I do with all that money. It seemed that a hidden benefit for being able to see over my belly was the growth of money in inverse proportion to the loss of calories. Not bad.

Two more weeks without my beloved French fries and I beheld a weight loss of six pounds and a cash growth of sixteen dollars. Well, I still couldn't fit into a sports car, but my modeling assignments were unaffected, and Terry had not noticed a difference. That was good, I didn't want Terry to feel insecure.

Winter came, which meant no snakes, and I rode along for a few months on the diet of one bacon-cheeseburger, one iced tea and one pint of ice cream three times a day. My weight held steady, and I still couldn't see below my stomach, but I had grown used to this amount of daily intake; didn't miss the extra burgers and stuff. So, when spring arrived with all its many snakes, and my ankle continued to swell as a reminder, and I still couldn't see down over my front, I realized again that I needed to re-think my situation.

What's more, while standing on Terry's patio, I had been stung twice by a scorpion. Though knowing that something was stinging my foot, I was helpless to see what it was, and had to ask Terry to look.

After an hour in the emergency clinic, able only to see in a mirror the red swells from scorpion damage, and when the examination table creaked and sagged under my load, causing the emergency physician some concern: he feared the table would break, and I sensed that he was more worried about the table than about me—I got my dander up.

Terry drove me home. During the ride, I thought: it's spring, more rattlers, couldn't see the scorpion at all, something had to go, probably more of my bulk. Possibly just a few more pounds would do the trick. All along I had said nothing to Terry about this dieting episode in my life. Actually I wouldn't call it a diet. It wasn't a scheme to overall lose weight. Not a diet at all. As I said, I didn't count calories. I just wanted to be able to see over better. Besides, Terry loved me just as I was. And, my career depended on me just as I was. And, there was the concern that should I again receive venom from another beast, the reaction would be more severe; not an event I wanted to repeat.

So I decided something else in the food category must be deleted. Do without bacon? I could still look forward to cheeseburgers.

But in time, omitting bacon made little difference, maybe a few ounces, and I, with grief in my heart, began to omit the cheese. Burgers without cheese?

I watched the cash grow, and realized I had so much more in the bank now I could buy more shares of Fat Fashions by Fabulous and Leviathan Ladies' Lingerie: big sites for big people. They also paid a sizable dividend.

Changes were taking place, for after four weeks without cheese, if I struggled I could just, almost, barely see the ground beneath my bulk. Other changes became clear as well, I noticed that I didn't miss the food I had reluctantly excluded, and, I was wealthier. Interesting. Terry's car seat fit better around me; I didn't roll up on its edges, and I was no longer in danger of preventing the car's airbags from functioning. Well, well.

Saints Be.

I had to buy more clothes. But I soon noticed that fewer observers were watching the photo shoots. Why was that?

I coasted along like this for another six weeks, but now, when I went to the gym to weigh, I walked. It was only one block, anyway. I had always felt good, whatever that was, but now I felt better. However, as my bank account and equities grew, and the pounds dropped due to more walking, I experienced the beginnings of a drop in modeling assignments. Big and oversized, it seemed, wasn't the same as obese. Didn't attract the same voyeurs. Fewer fashion houses wanted my photos. I was well-off though, wasn't at a loss for money, so it hardly registered.

Until more walking to the gym to weigh took off twenty more pounds, and the agency rarely called me. Though now I could see my feet, and that was a treat, I began to worry. Yes, I had money, but that wouldn't last forever. I began to see this being able to see my feet, see rattlers, see scorpions, as a mixed benefit: weight loss equated to job loss; job loss equated to starving; starving equated to not what I had in mind.

I thought about gaining back some of that weight, but, alas, I found that I just couldn't eat all that food these days. One day the effluvium wafting off a cheeseburger actually made me nauseous. My stomach must have really shrunk. What was worse was that I, without meaning to, began to eat less, and, slowly, more of less. My clothes didn't fit: looked on me like a tent collapsed in desert winds. Were not pretty. I had to order more outfits, but soon found that website oversized fashions were all too large. I began to shop at a brick-and-mortar. Was I happier? Well, I have always been happy, but now with the threat of no income, I began experiencing anxiety. My suspicions that, indeed, I was un-hirable began when Terry noticed. We were about to eat in a restaurant when the maître d' said the only seating available was a booth. I actually fit into a booth for the first time, but Terry didn't. We had to wait for our usual table. I was okay with that, but Terry was less happy with me now.

Trilby, my best marketer at my best agency in Manhattan, called to meet her for lunch.

"We have to talk," she said.

She looked across the lunch table at me.

"Something's different about you."

She scanned me with scrunch-down-lidded eyes.

"You've lost a lot. No wonder I've no requests for you. I called Fat" (as in Fat Fashions by Fabulous) "and they said you didn't fill out their fashions any more. I can see that for myself."

She continued to look me over.

"I know," I said. "I try to eat more, but sometimes food turns me off. And, I think I'll have what you're having; avocado with tomato."

Trilby shook her head. "No bacon cheeseburger?"

I pretended not to hear.

We ordered.

Even the avocado took its time going down. My stomach had shrunk daily, it seemed.

Trilby looked me over some more.

"Why don't you saunter over to the Ford Agency," she said.

I thought she was worried about losing the commissions I had brought in for the past few years.

"I'll call Eileen and set up an appointment for you. They might have catalogue work fit for you."

We ordered wine. (I forgot to mention that I still enjoyed wine, just not as many ounces as before.) The waiter poured and we toasted to my putting on a hundred pounds.

What catalogue work meant was that Trilby saw me as betwixt and between: too light for fat fashion, too heavy for high fashion. And, along with my size, my bank account was slimming down, and I didn't want to sell my equities, so I took Trilby's advice and found myself at the Ford Modeling Agency.

Ford indeed had work for me and soon, my lesser mass and pretty face appeared in such print as you get in the mail; you know, Penney's, Sears, Macy's, Target—those pulp flyers in your mailbox. The money was adequate. I had no complaints.

Terry called less and less. I knew he didn't like my bulking-down, but what could I do? I was out of control eating less and less, and walking more and more. Now, I found that it felt better to walk to the faraway gym to weigh, but the lower weight was so depressing that while there, I had to work off some of the anguish. If I tried pushing one of the machines, I thought, perhaps my distress would lessen. Thereafter, each night when I weighed, I played with some of the machines.

Buddhists say, "Everything changes, nothing remains." As I walked home after a few weeks using the gym, I felt the full impact of what they say: I received admiring glances—for me a big change. But I heard no more from Terry. Now, I bought eggs and broccoli; never bought french fries and pizza; absolutely couldn't abide a cheeseburger or ice-cream. I had to replace my entire wardrobe, and had no more modeling assignments. Even the pulp print found me lacking. Too thin. I thought of other work I might do: trimming dead leaves at a florist; cleaning bathrooms at H&R Block. Dreary. When I occasionally gave Terry a call to see what was up, he would say he had been out of town for his business, and he would get back to me. He didn't.

Trilby called for lunch. When I walked in, she looked right passed me. And when I sat at her table, her shock stiffened her rigid.

"Trilby, it's me. I know I've changed, but it's still me."

She swallowed hard. "I can see that . . . I wouldn't have known you. Had you died, and I was called in to identify you, I would have said, That's not Cleo."

The silence seemed to measure me while Trilby digested the new me.

"Trilby, I'm in danger of using my savings. I need to work. Is there nothing for me?" I was desperate.

She didn't reply. Just stared at me as I sat there worried. She took in my sculpted flawless skin and bones, flaxen hair. I know I was a shock. I couldn't tell you how much weight I was down.

Finally Trilby spoke.

"Have you been to Ford lately?"

"No. When modeling assignments dried up, I stopped going in. I haven't been there in months."

"Well, go. Go tomorrow. Don't wait. Ask for Eileen. Don't talk to anyone else. I'll call her to make sure she will be there."

She said nothing more and we continued to enjoy lunch. She ordered a salad and I had poached eggs. It was quite strange the way she kept looking at me.

After the loss of so much good work, I had little hope that anyone would again want me to model. But Trilby had always been helpful and I didn't want to ignore her advice. The next day, as soon as I entered Ford's door, Eileen was ready and waiting for me. She looked me up and down, swallowed hard (these agents seem to have a knack for hard swallowing), took me into her inner office, called a few numbers while I waited, gave me an address and told me to be at that place immediately. Was I in trouble? Were they so irritated that I had lost so much weight that they had some kind of ridicule in store? Anyway, I walked the few blocks to the designated address and in the door. What met me were six photographers, tongues hanging out, eyes rounded into astonished circles, cameras at the ready.

"Cleo, please stand over here," someone said. And I did—cameras going off all around. Someone said, "Vogue." I played the part, but I thought he must have meant 'vague.' They encrusted me with makeup, gave me hats, scarves, spiked heels, and exotic apparel to change into. They asked me to act out funny positions. I couldn't imagine whatever for, until later when the money started coming in; much more than I had ever seen before.

Trilby called to say that I must get the next issue of Vogue. She said I was the latest sensation in high-fashion models. I could command thousands per shoot. She said she was dancing up and down with glee and a fat commission. "Fat," a long-time-ago-word that I never heard now, except regarding commissions and checks.

I bought Vogue, and there I was on the cover, large as life (which was now quite small). I had had no idea. Some would say a shadow of my former self, but I don't think I would have cast a shadow. The Ford Agency had assignments lined up for me around the world for the next year and beyond. Everyone wanted me to pose, and now, once again, people came to watch.

Saints be.

Happy to be working again, I rarely thought about Terry, but I did miss him.

After about six months I had an assignment that put me into the arms of a captivating man. I thought he looked slightly familiar, but he wore a slim tuxedo and had a thin little black mustache, and I had never been out with a tuxedo-mustached man. With his slicked-back black hair, crisp, strong jaw, I was slightly confused by his familiar look. The designers had dressed me in glossy satins with diamond studs in my piled-up twisted hair. It had taken an age to get me outfitted and painted up. I wore platform sandals and the make-up artist had painted my toenails blue. I was a sight. The photographer had us incline on a carved, silk, ermine-trimmed, gold studded chaise longue, and told the handsome man to put his arm around me. His arm felt so good. So familiar. I stared hard into his face; the photographer didn't care what we did, as long as we kept close and touching.

"Terry?" He stared back at me. "It's me, Terry. Cleo. Where've you been? What happened to you?"

"Cleo! It's actually you, Cleo! You're gorgeous! After you changed, I had been so afraid to call you; so afraid you wouldn't love me ever again. I couldn't eat. I couldn't sleep. I started walking to work off the anxiety. After months I decided to take a chance and call you, and since your number no longer answered I stopped by your agency."

The photographer didn't care if we talked as long as we gazed into each other's eyes. This was easy to do. We shifted positions on the carved, silk, ermine-trimmed, gold studded, chaise longue. Terry put his other arm around me, and continued.

"Trilby took one look at me and sent me over to Ford. I walked in and the rest is history. Here I am.

As soon as we get out of here, let's go buy a sports car."

Saints be

## Quantum Mercy

Robert hardly sees the passing fields as he drives down the long, straight, country road. His mind is tucked far inside like a meditating monk's. The road stretches as far as he can see and requires so little attention that he can almost set the BMW on autopilot and nod off. He listens to the quiet. Other than some disquieting memories he would like a chance to revisit and correct, not much bothers him now, and he feels light about where he is going, and why.

Now, as the BMW gains distance, one of those long-suppressed regrets moves into Robert's consciousness. What mysterious force pulls up those unsummoned memories, he wonders.

\* \* \*

This one's about the time when Laura, begged him to leave right then so she could say goodbye to her father before he died. Instead, Robert had replied that before he could leave, he had to give his attention to a legal case. Eventually they did leave.

The video in his head played the arrival scene. Laura was at the door with her father's butler bearing the news that her father was gone. He had died but ten minutes earlier. Robert heard this news while taking their bags from the car's trunk. After that, Laura closed off from him; blamed him: the sadness, the closure firmly in her bones.

\* \* \*

Why does that scene appear to him now; surface randomly? It was eleven years ago and buried. Still it's a memory he wishes he could alter.

Then as he continues to stare down the long road, his reverie is broken by the arrival of a presence in the passenger seat. He turns his head and sees Laura.

"Please hurry," she says. "I must tell dad I love him."

Robert wakes up to her fear and hits the throttle. When they arrive he removes bags from the car trunk, and sees the butler's large smile as he welcomes Laura. He hears the butler say, "Your father is sitting up in bed eager to welcome you." They have made it in good time.

\* \* \*

The road comes up, disappears, comes up, disappears. Robert is transfixed. He thinks about Willy, the kitty, whom he had let out the door, not realizing the kitty would not return; not knowing it would venture into the road; after all, their garden was extensive. He recalls standing at the window and seeing Willy flattened on the street: something else he would change.

But nothing changes on the road ahead; that view might as well be wallpaper. Perhaps it's been wallpaper all along—road, fields, sky, which the great wall-paperer tweaks each second. He read once, that God had to recreate the universe every instant.

\* \* \*

As he looked at torn wallpaper, he seemed to be back in his old house. He would have to re-paper this room. The rickety old Victorian was his and Laura's first home; all he could afford as a beginning associate in the law firm of Pearce, Pardon and Prattle.

Willy wants out.

"I'll show you where your new litter-box is, Willy; you'll become quite accustomed to it. It's dangerous for you out there."

* * *

Nothing—no bump, no bend—breaks up the road ahead. The passing green fields are lovely to distraction. Willy's presence next to him, fast asleep on the passenger's seat connects Robert to his own humanity. Willy is nearly seven now, and a fine pet. Robert reaches over and pets Willy. The BMW rolls on and Robert focuses down the endless straight road. But his reverie is interrupted by a memory of the time their poodle, Oscar, contributed to the Johnsons' St. Bernard being killed.

* * *

The dogs had been playing, but Oscar was up in the Johnsons' driveway and the St. Bernard ran before the mail truck. The Johnsons' hearts must have been broken. Robert and Laura should at least have replaced the dog for them; should have offered to, but St. Bernards were expensive, and in those early days, Robert and Laura were living on a beginning associate's salary—in debt a bit—no dollars left in any pay period. They hadn't offered. This omission had stuck to him like iron filings to a magnet.

* * *

Is this road magnetized? The BMW attached to it forever? Strangely it seems to be alive somehow—to grimace with him, to smile with him, to breathe with him.

52

He looks out the window and sees the Johnson's house. Whenever Oscar is let out, he usually comes right back into the house, preferring to be with the family. But this time Robert sees Oscar trot up the hill to the Johnsons. Their St. Bernard is out, and he and Oscar are great friends, cavort all over. Robert opens the door and calls, "Oscar! Come on, Oscar." Robert whistles. Oscar obeys. Ears flapping, he flies down the road and into the house. The mail truck passes on by without incident. "Oscar, you're a good dog. Come, Oscar. Sit here on the couch by me. I'm happy to have you, Oscar, and today I bought your favorite food. Later, you and I will throw and fetch sticks at the beach."

\* \* \*

That was four years ago, and now Oscar stretches across the back seat of the BMW. Oscar loves to be on the road. Thank you, Laura, for leaving Oscar. "Something to love. Something to love." Has he said that aloud? For Oscar stands up and winks at him in the rearview mirror. Robert feels less heavy; his memories are lighter now.

This is a strange road, somehow seems unreal, makes him feel that he, Willy, and Oscar are only half real. He has never taken this road before: the back way, the way to his interview in the small town of Peace Valley. His first interview after two rejections; after he had been dismissed from Pearce, Pardon and Prattle. He must try to stay awake, pet Willy and Oscar now and then. He tries the radio but finds nothing to tolerate, and from too frequent use, his CDs only irritate. Actually, he likes the quiet. The BMW has a special hum. It begins to sound like the first notes of Sibelius's *First*.

Sibelius: that brings up a memory

\* \* \*

Laura had wanted to attend that performance at Carnegie Hall.

"I would never drive into the city." he had said. "The old Mercedes won't survive. Even in a guarded lot, when we return to it, parts will be missing."

Laura's mouth scowled into disappointment.

"You can go in on the train," he had said. "The last train out of the city doesn't leave until 12:00, and the symphony ends in time for you to get that train home."

"I tried that once for the ballet," she said, "but afterward I couldn't get a cab, and had a fearsome lonely walk to Grand Central. Alone. I won't do that again. You could come on the train with me," she pleaded.

"No." And he had turned his head to the brief he needed to compile for the next court case.

* * *

He would treat her request differently now; if he could. He brings his mind back to the endless road; it never varies

But now he can't see the road for he is at Symphony Hall and hears Sibelius rise up, swell, filling him. Life throbs in the drums, the tympani. Laura holds his hand. He turns to see excitement glow in her face. He has carefully taken seats for them in the middle of the first balcony. Prime. Worth a day's salary, but so is it to see her glow. And the Mercedes—well, that might take some C-notes to fix, and they may have to hire a limo to take them home, but the symphony is renewing their energy. When the percussions strike, his elation is such he could almost leap out of his seat and soar over the concert hall.

When they arrive home, Laura says, "Thank you for this wonderful evening. Sibelius must be my favorite composer."

After work the next day he buys a Sibelius CD for her. For days afterward, Laura talks about that evening. Tells her friends. Robert feels as much like a hero as any man can.

*　*　*

On the road, Robert sees no other vehicle. No party animals out here.

Then, strangely, he remembers the sign on his neighbors' door: *Support wildlife. Throw a party.* Those neighbors, Jane and Earl Bruin, with their exuberant chirpiness—he had had a bad time with Laura about them.

Periodic screams would rise up from the neighbors' direction.

"What is all that screaming about next door?" he had asked Laura.

"Jane 's practicing Primal Therapy. You try to relive your passage through the birth canal; a painful process that her psychologist thinks shaped her life."

"Criminy! And . . . ."

"The reliving and screaming is supposed to center one away from the birth pain . . . thus fewer neuroses."

He remembered how he had acted when Laura invited the Bruins to a party: he had thought he would have some fun.

"I've heard your screams, Jane," he had said. "They're perfectly delightful, especially when I'm concentrating on a brief."

Jane looked pleased, but Robert had caught the dagger that Earl's eyes flashed. Especially provoking was Jane's cackle. So—undeterred, despite Earl's glare—Robert continued.

"Watch out everyone, Jane's about to hatch an egg!" he said.

Earl scowled. "You don't have to be rude."

Robert found a chair and nodded off. Laura didn't forgive him for days.

He wished he could have partied with them, but he had grown catatonic waiting for the egg. He had had no regrets about that. Well—maybe he had—if he could be sure it would be the last time they had a party, or at least the last time to have the Bruins over, he might have had the patience enough to be less cynical.

*  *  *

Is that a mirage on the road up ahead? He sees a festive party in progress.

"Jane, have another hors d'oeuvre," Robert says, and he passes the plate to her. "She has the most beautiful laugh, Earl. What a joy it must be to live with such a woman. Don't you have to take some kind of uppers to keep up with her?" he asks. "And her scream reaches a beautiful note . . . high C, isn't it? It's thrilling . . . gets me going . . . Maria Callas . . . right next door. Laura and I are happy to have you two for neighbors."

He sees that Laura is pleased with him. It takes so little.

*  *  *

Keep focused on the taut road. It stretches ahead plain and pure. He stares down it warily as though finally, it may be a rubber band that earth will release, letting it snap back. Taut road reminds him of that last tort.

Case 23-891 had required extensive research: finding precedent, locating witnesses and deposing them; finding in his budget the funds to fly them in. He had worked days and nights on that, along with compiling briefs. Thanks to the Internet, some of the evening work had been done at home. Laura often helped. Sometimes he had written in longhand, and she had typed the results into his laptop. He had

56

grown to rely on her help. She had appeared happy to help, and he had taken her out for a special candlelight dinner at least once a week. What had she done with the rest of her time? He couldn't have said. Due to work demands ("lawyer" is a euphemism for "slave"), he had come in from work very late most nights and asked, and she usually said, Oh nothing much.

How had those briefs for Case 23-891 gone missing? They were on the laptop until the day before the trial. The jury had been chosen, and lawyers and witnesses were ready. At home that night, he had opened the laptop to print the final documents, but had been unable to find Case 23-891. Surely he had been looking in the wrong directory. Had the files been moved? This memory plagued him.

He attempts to concentrate on the road, but it is so straight and silent. No obstacles like Case 23-891.

\* \* \*

"Laura, I have a problem," he had called out.

She came into the room and said nothing. Her serious look matched his.

"I can't find the briefs for Case 23-891. Did you move them? Did you work on them today, or even yesterday? Can you help? I'm down to the wire now."

He rose, and Laura sat at the laptop. She clicked this and that, scanned directories, windows appeared, disappeared. "You've got me," she had said. "Didn't you copy them for your computer at work?" She was cool, unconcerned.

"No," he had said. His throat tightened. "I thought there was something yet to be added today . . . that last testimony.

"Well, the last time I used those files," she said, "they were fine, and located as usual under the case number."

He had been ruined. As the lead attorney on the case, without those briefs, he had stumbled, presented flimsy, unacceptable arguments. He had not had the required witness backgrounds or questions for them, and he was bound to lose the case. His attempts were laughable. His company was not pleased; they would possibly lose millions.

Early in the case he had daily transferred the files from his home computer to the company's at work. But much had been done at home, and Laura had said she had data to add, thus he had not made that transfer in the last two days. A deadly lapse of attention. Even though he had stayed up all night trying to recover the research needed to present at trial, he had mangled the case.

Fix on the road. There have been no signs for Peace Valley. The road lulls him, but still the missing briefs rise up in his consciousness: all that good work, where did it go?

* * *

He sees Laura at the computer, trying to retrieve the lost documents. She does not appeared concerned—not frantic as he is. She turns to him.

"I don't give a shit about your work," she says. "That documentation is your problem. It's all been driving me to insanity: the boredom, the soul-stifling boredom." She slams down the mouse and stands. "Figure it out for yourself," she shouts. "I'm out of here!"

* * *

Long after it was far too late to help, he had taken the laptop to a computer store to see if they could find the missing files, ten in all, and determine how they had been deleted. The technician found that, indeed, all ten had been deleted—deleted by LC420—Laura.

In the first days of the trial, the Grand Fromages at Pearce, Pardon and Prattle had watched, stunned.

Robert had been one of their best. Robert had been such a fast-rising legal mind—yet; they had dismissed him from the Firm. He had had no recourse.

Laura had left him with surprising speed. For days in disbelief, he had wandered the large home. Willy and Oscar seemed to understand; followed him around. Thank God, Laura left the animals. She had not left much else. She knew exactly what she wanted to take, as though she had planned it. The movers had moved in and whoosh—she had moved out. He had a table and chair and couch and bed and TV and litter-box. Aside from plenty of cat and dog food, that was about it.

Well, he won't continue to feel regret about that memory; aside from failing to back up the files, he himself had done no harm.

\* \* \*

The infinite road appears to expand; seems to move into another dimension. Perhaps for miles, he has been in another dimension.

The position, for which he is to interview with a law firm at the road's end in the town of Peace Valley, is small town stuff: boundary disputes, dog bites, wills, divorces. He will hardly earn enough to keep up the BMW. Best to trade that in so as not to intimidate the locals. He is expecting a situation he wants; he does not want his old high-pressure practice, and is looking toward a different kind of practice.

He sees nothing ahead at the road's end. Large at the junction of the BMW, the road disappears ahead to a massless point. Funny about perspective, he muses—how it changes so rapidly: here large, there tiny. He vaguely understands the process, but how fast it happens, nevertheless, is profound to the point that it affects his life: issues or problems that loom up large are not seen on the horizon. It's only when space-time brings them in close that they can be seen for what they are. Sometimes too late.

On arrival in Peace Valley, he'll take a room in the one motel he has found on the Internet; kind of a mom and pop place. Then, if he lands the position, he'll look around for a cottage or apartment to rent, with a garden for his four-footed family. The house back east is for sale. Everything he owns is in his car's trunk; moving in will be easy, take only half an hour. The owner of the law firm that waits for Robert in Peace Valley, Mr. McCaffey, is elderly and wants to retire in a few years; wants a partner to replace him and keep the firm going, someone who will enjoy a small rural practice. If Robert lands the position, and if he works some at home, Robert promises himself to back up everything on the laptop each night. Two copies. Then he will take one copy to work and file the other at home. He feels lighter about swapping the high-pressure, all-consuming career, for a gentler one. He, Willy, and Oscar ride in silence, mesmerized by the BMW's hum.

* * *

A vision comes up of the straight-eight Oldsmobile Robert once owned. He had helped his nephew, David, who attended college in Boston; helped him with finances. When he told David that he would come up for a visit, David had warned him to come up in the big, old, yellow straight-eight Olds. Car theft was rampant in Boston, David had said, but no one would steal *that* car.

At dinner, David had asked whether he might buy the Olds. They had laugh over that idea. He' would like to drive out in the country occasionally, he said. Robert said no; it would cost too much to keep in Boston. Now he wishes he could go back, give David the Olds.

\* \* \*

He finds that he can't see the road or his creature friends, nor does he hear the BMW's hum. He sits aside David at the oyster bar in the Union Oyster House, and they slurp down oysters as fast as the bartender can shuck them.

David stops for a breath and asks, "Uncle Robert, how about letting me have the Olds? I can pay you for it when I find a job. You know I'll be finished with my Master's this term, and already have interviews scheduled." He gulps another oyster.

Robert, busy with his own oyster, listens. Says nothing.

"I'd like to take my girlfriend for a ride," David says.

Robert wipes his chin and gives David a hard look. For a minute David thinks the answer will be no.

"What a splendid idea, David. Take it off my hands . . . I won't have to keep it up. Sometimes it's just in the way. Tomorrow let's find a motor-vehicle bureau and transfer the title. You'll have the expenses to manage, though. Let me know if you need help with those."

Robert feels as good as a man who has dog and cat companions, and who has done a thoughtful deed—can feel.

\* \* \*

He'd better stop and walk Oscar, and also Willy, if he will. First he puts a leash on Oscar and takes him out to relieve himself. While he waits, he listens to the quiet fields; the stillness is almost eerie. Nothing moves, not even a cloud; the sky is a clear blue bubble. What kind of place is this? No aromas to inhale.

He pictures Claire, the woman he had learned to love while working with her. Though she had returned his love, they had kept temptation at bay.

Oscar hops back into the car, wants to be safe, not loose in the unknown. Robert puts a harness on Willy and lifts him out. But Willy is too scared, thank you. The litter box will work fine, when I'm ready. With both animals, companions, back safely in the BMW, it rolls on down the road. In all this time they have seen nothing mechanical, and have seen nothing alive and moving—except for fields; and even they are still.

Now the road disappears at the end into a web. A web? A web of Robert's weaving? He recalls that Claire's, hobby was weaving, and once, when she had worked with Robert on the Philmore case, she wore a scarf that she had woven. He remembers the scent of her on the scarf. Actually, in time, they fell into something more than working. When they accidentally touched, electricity coursed around the room until it was embarrassing. Once, after working many nights at the office, they had had dinner together—a memory he will always cherish. Then she had asked him to come by her house for a nightcap. He did. After that, they cooled it—they loved each other but timing was wrong: Robert had a wife, and besides, partners' fraternizing was against company policy. By the time Laura had left him, Claire had moved on to another law firm. He wishes he could sense Clair's perfume now; he deeply misses her.

\* \* \*

Peace Valley. He has an interview coming up in the little town of Peace Valley. He hopes to win the position and looks forward to the easy pace. His eyes meet the road. There have been no signs for Peace Valley—but are there buildings emerging far ahead? He turns to check on Oscar and Willy, both now in the back seat; Willy's head rests on Oscar's thigh.

Robert is surprised to find that he can sense Clair's perfume filling the car.

"And, anyway," he says out loud, "Who with a good legal brain would consent to living and working in Peace Valley? That is . . . if I land the position."

But he is teasing, for he is light-hearted, confident, and eager for the change.

"Except you guys of course. And except you, Claire. I trust that you've examined your head . . . better yet your motives."

"For the longest time," she says.

He takes her hand and together they look ahead toward the buildings, and toward their future, down the long road.

# Lately I'm Not Myself

L ately it's been hard to find
    time for chores I have to do
I haven't been
        myself
            and that has caused a certain
busyness in trying to discover
        who I am

What if I am someone else?
        how disconcerting to learn
I may be
        someone else
not who I think
        I am

I slouched back onto the bed and
        got up on a different side,
but still I wasn't myself and
        who?

Lately I'm Not Myself

There're too many similar
    souls
to examine and to decide
    am I you?

No. I could never see
    myself
        in a red hat and yellow dress
            you must be someone
                else
I hope you do know
    who

It would be too chaotic
    to have many of us trying to find
ourselves
    wondering how we were
        deceived into thinking we were
            who
we thought we were
    all that time

Anyway, last Monday
    I met someone who was surely
        me
            or was I surely
                she?
she looked wise and well-together
    put

I was about to accost her for taking my
    consciousness
        and about to insist she accept
            who
I am now
    it's been a bad fit

But when I saw her with
    three ornery teenagers
        I quickly realized I erred
in thinking she could be
    me

You see how challenging it can
    be
not to be
    yourself

In trying to narrow the range of those who might
    be me
I listed attributes and skills I wished for
    me to be

This kept me from watching
    every gal and wondering whether
        I was she
            and from asking her
if she wasn't really
    herself

With my list in mind I took
    timeout to daydream about
who I might in fact
    be

Or, given choice, who I wanted
    to be
        and to wonder whenever did
            this disconnect
happen?
    the supermarket is the
        one place in this small town to look
            so off to there I went

First I scanned the parking lot for cars I like
    here was a sharp gal loading a sleek coupe
        aha!
she could be
    me

(Or I could be she) but no, I watched as
    she  loaded her car
        she had bought
            Cool Whip and fake mayonnaise
                I choked just imagining it
she could never be
    me

I soon exhausted parking lot potential
    I knew I only liked coupes
        I knew that about
myself
    whoever I was
and so I headed into the
    supermarket

I zeroed in on a gal who was with the perfect guy
    she was
who I was
    I knew
        until I heard him speaking
French

If she were really me I would need
    to learn more French
        it's one thing to rattle it off,
but two things to
    understand

Even though I looked wonderful as
    she

it might spoil my love to know what he
was saying
so no she must not be
me

You see what I am up against

I'll keep working on this mystery
even though it's dawned on
me
that whoever I am
I'll give thinks for
whoever this is.

# The Chinese Herb Cure

"Aren't you worried about your neighbors? It's eleven and they're probably trying to sleep . . . lights are off." Pete had the volume loud enough to hurt Susan's ears.

"Nah. They're fine . . . doesn't bother them." Pete kept dancing; feeling the rhythm, his nimble form swaying like a willow branch in a breeze.

"Maybe you should at least shut the window," Susan said, as she bobbed and gyrated to the energetic beat, determined to wear a smile, not spoil the evening. She wore her skinny jeans and knew that she looked terrific. She had a sense that everything was good—except for the loud music. Can he really not mind that he's blasting the entire neighborhood, she wondered. And the neighbor's house is barely thirty feet away.

Pete danced over and shut the window.

They moved separately, never touching. Susan loved to watch Pete's lean body and fluid moves. At those times he always had a smile for her.

* * *

Time was when they danced often. But those nights were over, for Pete was not feeling well. It was his stomach.

Frequently he said, "After I eat, I feel bloated, impacted, swollen. It's hard to describe, but it's not a good feeling." Most of the time he kept a hand on his abdomen, as though he could sooth away the problem. His face was set into a perpetual worried frown. There was no more dancing and scarcely any laughing. The days and nights were now fragile and filled with unease.

"I think you need to see a physician," Susan would say when Pete would open up about his discomfort. "You need to be seen by a gastroenterologist, or whomever." She had said this too often.

But Pete followed another source of advice: Jane. Jane had once been Pete's employer when she and her husband, Clyde, had owned Massage Magazine. Jane specialized in Chinese herbs.

"On my last bike ride with Jane and Clyde, he told me how the herbs Jane came up with were helping his chest pains. Jane said any ailment could be cured if only one had the right herb, or potion. She is certain that my problem is an allergy or sensitivity that can be cured with one of her herbs." Although Pete hoped to convince Susan, he would anyway do as he wished. "Jane has done extensive study. Apparently the Chinese have cures that most of the West hasn't heard about. Jane thinks it's a shame our doctors don't get some training in China."

So Pete was on schedule to try several of Jane's herbs, alternating them until he felt better, less bloated. For this, Jane had supplied him with small brown bottles of solution accompanied by instructions—so many drops of this one, so many

70

drops of that one. And, he had to eliminate certain foods, one at a time, until he identified the culprit. Jane also instructed Pete to practice meditation. Actually, he had been doing so for years now—so that would not be a change.

Susan didn't trust Jane's recommendations. "What if it's something serious and you're letting it thrive?"

"Jane really knows her stuff, Sweets," Pete said. "The proof is in how her herbs have reduced Clyde's chest pains."

"Well, your problem came on so gradually. I think an allergy that serious would have flared quickly . . . not dragged out so."

He did not reply.

Susan continued to watch the steaming rice and broccoli. It would only annoy Pete, make things worse, if she told him what she really thought of Jane and her ideas. Pete's faith in Jane was puzzling. Jane wore long thick hair, which every five minutes she would flip around in flirtatious self-awareness, stroking and draping hunks of it over her chest. Not too odd—had she been sixteen—but Jane was in her early fifties.

"It's your karma to have this problem," Jane said. She used the word "karma" in every third sentence. She had trouble delivering her sentences without using the word "karma." Everything good and everything bad depended on karma. There was no talking to Jane without the feeling that she wasn't listening. And, aside from informing people about Chinese herbs, she regaled them with how she spent days enduring the outline of a full tree, all its bare branches, being tattooed on her back. Her entire back. She would go topless at home to show it off.

\* \* \*

Rice and broccoli, and sometimes bananas and eggs: that was the diet to which Pete and Susan were limited. That was all he could eat, and even with that—eating small amounts—he would suffer a bloated, stuffed feeling. He could not be distracted from his discomfort. For Pete, everything had better be in its place, but he couldn't find a place in which to be better.

"Jane has me taking schizandra fruits and licorice roots. Also astragalus and rhubarb. Rhubarb!! And she thinks I may be allergic to wheat, so bread is out—no cake or cookies. No milk products. I have to eliminate those," he told Susan. Constant anxiety pushed him to cruise the room, always with a hand on his abdomen.

Susan nodded agreement. She didn't think Pete and Jane were on the right track, but she had asked him to see a specialist too many times now, and he had resisted, preferring to believe Jane (with a perfect herb and diet just around the corner). Susan just about gave up. She wanted to keep peace with Pete, and her comments weren't helping.

So they shopped for rice flour, rice milk, rice crackers, rice cakes, any rice product, and Jell-O. Susan had a difficult time putting together a meal. Meals were frustrating anyway; Pete could eat so little—a few bites and the stuffed feeling would begin.

"Liquids go down easily. That's puzzling," he said. Once virile, strong and lean, he was losing too much weight: measurable changes were daily taking place in him. Each day Susan thought he looked worse.

"Something is very wrong and I hope Jane will figure it out soon." He was always quoting Jane.

Jane, Jane, Susan routinely bobbed her head in support, as though it were on a hinge with a chain being yanked from another universe. She was out of words.

Pete also ingested a steady diet of Tums and Pepto-Bismol, drinking it straight from a bottle that he kept in the fridge. Not getting relief from these, he tried Milk of Magnesia and various stool softeners. He meditated. He prayed. His anxiety mounted and he took anxiety medication. Somewhere around the corner awaited his cure. He just had to have faith and patience and try another herb. His misery was taking a toll on his and Susan's young marriage.

"It's increasingly difficult to live this way, Pete. Without knowing, without resolution, without a professional opinion. You think, if you try to ignore the discomfort, the problem will go away . . . clear itself up." Susan decided to go for broke, "Either you get yourself off to a real doctor, or I'm out-a-here," she said.

"You find one for me then. I don't know where to go," he yelled.

"I will!" she yelled back. But she didn't know any doctors. Didn't know who that should be.

In silence they ate their dinner of rice and Jell-O, Pete worrying about what was wrong, Susan worrying about the responsibility he had just put on her of finding the best doctor for him. What if he didn't like the doctor she found? What if something serious was wrong? What if the doctor screwed up? What if Jane had the power after all—could come up with the magic potion after Susan had put Pete through invasive medical exams?

The next day, Susan got the best referral for Pete she could get, and made his appointment. Then she moved out. Actually, moving out doesn't exactly describe what happened, since she hadn't yet moved in, and as they had not been married long, she still had her own house nine miles away. She decided to ditch Pete's complications and sleep at her house for a while. It wasn't that she wanted to desert Pete—she wanted to desert Jane. Jane's influence was wedging a crevice into their marriage. Susan didn't issue an ultimatum to Pete; she just left, saying, I'll be back at the house. Call me when you need me."

Pete let a few days go by without calling Susan. He had had Jane drive him to the tests; he wanted to punish Susan for desertion. But when the critical hour came to hear the findings, he wanted Susan with him.

Sweets," Pete spoke to Susan over the phone, The tests results are in, and I have to see Dr. Yin this afternoon to go over them. Jane drove me for the tests . . . they require that . . . you aren't allowed to go home alone. But, I want you to be with me today . . . if you will."

Pete and Susan faced Dr. Yin across his desk and waited to hear his findings.

The passageway that empties the contents of your stomach into your colon is closing up," said the doctor. Actually it is nearly closed. I have to go in and reopen it. It should be a fairly simple operation." He drew diagrams to demonstrate what he had found.

Susan felt enormous relief. Pete could only find as much relief as the thought of upcoming surgery would allow.

I'll schedule the operation right away," Dr. Yin said.

On their drive home Pete didn't know how to feel. He had gone through a lot to get to this point, x-rays, endoscopy, enemas, and blood tests. He hoped it wasn't all winding up to something dire.

I finally feel good about it," Susan said. I have faith. The surgery will work and you'll feel good

74

again. We'll dance, act silly, and laugh again. You'll be able to eat normally. I've missed you."

* * *

Two days later, Susan watched helplessly as the orderlies strapped Pete down on the gurney, ready to take him to surgery.

"You'll be just fine. Dr. Yin is tops and highly recommended. The other doctor I told you about said he knew several people whom Dr. Yin had operated on and who were very satisfied with him."

Several hours later Dr. Yin came from surgery to tell Susan about his findings.

"Pete is recovering nicely. There was a closure on the passage out of the stomach and I've opened it up," he said. "There was no cancer. I don't know what caused the closure. Maybe it was congenital and had just decided to take this year to grow. I can't possibly guess why."

"Just his karma," Susan could imagine Jane saying. She stayed with Pete to help him heal and, after all, he was her husband. Unfortunately now, slicing down his beautiful lean and fit abdomen, was a long ugly scar. Though he didn't say, she knew that Pete, being quite vain, and always working-out to look good, must have hated his scar. Well, what can you do? she thought.

Pete's healing progressed. He gave up all strange, prohibitive diets and once more enjoyed both his and Susan's home-cooked and varied dinners. He just had to take it easy, eat lightly for six weeks or so, and not lift more than ten pounds. He was careful to comply. He didn't experience bloating again. Susan enjoyed cooking, flourishing again in the kitchen. She spent less time at her house, and more time at Pete's. Maybe it *was* a good marriage. She had no "I told you so's" for Pete, which would cause him embarrassment that he had ignored her suspicions. A

75

different person now, he could hardly remember how lost he had felt.

"My stomach came very close to closing completely. Looking back, I can't see how I got through those difficult days. I was suffocating. Now I can breathe. And enjoy food. Even the light meals we have are a feast." Without saying so, he knew that Jane's Chinese herb routine had been a potentially dangerous detour, and without comment, the small brown bottles disappeared.

\* \* \*

"Clyde died!" Jane sobbed over the phone to Pete. "He was on his long bike ride, collapsed and suddenly died." This was stunning news. Clyde had been so fit—a marathon runner and cyclist. Strong.

"He had a heart attack!" Jane cried. "The past few weeks he *had* had some chest pains." Without thinking of the implications, Jane explained that she had treated Clyde's chest pains with special Chinese herbs. "He did so well on those herbs, and listen to this . . . he also had leukemia. No one knew . . . they just found out. They said the leukemia starved his heart of oxygen, causing his chest pains and heart attack."

When Pete related this news to Susan, they stood fixed, staring at each other, the tragedy dawning. The unspoken *what ifs*. The realization: had Clyde gone to a doctor to treat his leukemia, he would probably still be alive and enjoying life.

"There, but for you, go I . . . in a sense," Pete said to Susan.

Clyde might have lived. He wouldn't have had a heart attack, Susan thought, were it not for Chinese herbs.

"Why didn't he go for a professional opinion?" Susan asked.

"I guess we know the answer to that," Pete said.

Although Pete could eat normally now and was feeling safe again, and even happy—something was not right with his incision. He asked Susan to take a look. Sure enough it was bulging out. Very strange. The scar sported a regular swelling. A balloon of firm flesh.

"That doesn't look right, I agree." Susan stirred the pot she was tending on the stove. She felt dread. She so much wanted everything to be right for a while; at least most things. "We need to have Dr. Yin look at that. I'll make an appointment with him first thing in the morning," she said.

"I'm really surprised at this," said Dr. Yin.

Pete had his shirt pulled up exposing the prominent bulge in the long scar.

"And you're so young and fit. I would never have expected a hernia like this from the surgery. I'll have to go in and repair it."

\* \* \*

While in the hospital for the second time, Pete met someone else. Someone new. He didn't understand what had happened. Maybe it was just that with these scars marring his abdomen he needed a new woman: one who had not known how flat and ripped his abdomen had once been, and who didn't know how long he had been sold down a river of Chinese herbs.

And, she loved to dance.

# The Mannequin

While she half-listened to the banter of her children's store employees, Claire and Alex, Jill gazed out into the festive mall, sparkling with Christmas lights.

"A half-hour 'til closing and I need to duck out five minutes early to get to the cleaners," Claire said. "I have a hot date tonight, and need to pick up my hot dress."

"When's that guy going to pop the question?" Alex said. "After all you've known him a week now."

"Don't you mean a week of Sundays?" Claire said. "If he doesn't pop the question soon, I'll be popping him a question."

"And what's that?"

"Whether he'd rather sleep with me or sleep in the doghouse."

"Oh, really. I didn't know you had a doghouse," Alex said. "I hope it's a large one, for if I forget to get a pizza on my way home tonight, I'll need a doghouse to sleep in, and we don't have one. And what's your night-life lineup, Jill?" Alex asked. "I guess you're cooking for a date, as usual."

"That's true.

"Before we close," Jill continued, "I want to browse a couple shops. Don't lock up. I'll be back before you leave." She left Alex and Claire, to mind the store.

Along the mall concourse, she window-shopped, scanning luxuries and necessities, searching the faces of last minute shoppers, wondering about their situation: were they happy, were they disappointed, were they in union with someone, or were they quite alone.

The mall, almost empty now, seemed to amplify Jill's isolation. She passed a window with a display of table linens—place mats with Christmas patterns in red and green. On the mats stood candlesticks and funny crooked glasses. People bought those mats to brighten meals for the two or three in their family; or bought those funny glasses for their child's milk; or maybe a few candles for dinner with their husband or lover; those people who belonged with them. Unless, of course, they were alone.

The approach of closing time urged the remaining shoppers onward at a quicker pace. Their haste spread a fearful solidness about it that almost touched Jill.

In a pigeonhole shop, Jill saw, hunched behind the cash register, an overstuffed fake fur wrapped bear-like around a sales clerk who stared out defiantly, all pretense of salesmanship over for this evening. Meanwhile the clerk waited impatiently to clear the last counter of jewels. She scowled at Jill. Don't dare enter!

In the department store, Jill's thoughts wandered aimlessly from scene to scene. She stopped to sample hand crème—too strongly scented, she placed it back into its beribboned basket. Most jewelry had been swept from counters; hidden from unknown midnight viewers. Jill absorbed the mall's encroaching solitude, but hoping for something less detached, she turned toward the escalator, stepped on and rose up with it. She lurched off into mounds of smiling teddy bears, and moved on passed freaky, knee-high ceramic elephant tables. She shook her head, as if to a companion, and walked on toward the china. Here, counting checks and money, a pretty, young clerk flirted with a grinning red-faced young man. They paid Jill no attention while she watched. She felt invisible to the couple. Even the glistening china dishes seemed to look, knowing but silent, while they began their wait for the unbroken peace of night. All merchandise waited for another day.

No one was around now. Closing time stillness pervaded every item. The flooring seemed unyielding to pedestrians. Jill felt keenly alone—an invader who could stretch out on one of the beds coming into view and not be noticed until morning, if then.

She fancied she would see ghostly shoppers materializing to gawk and comment on amazing things they no longer needed. "My! That fancy jeweled dress, the likes of which my times never saw." Or, "That shirt would be perfect for my nephew in California." Jill imagined how they would waft in and out of visibility, hovering near the ceiling.

Back on the first floor, Jill passed the closed Steak House. The door looked boarded up. It seemed to have slammed in her face. Television sets nearby were still anxiously broadcasting their strident racket. "Look! We want to show you this," they cried out.

She passed over the shiny new parquet floor—one-eighth of an inch thick. She had seen it being installed. Take away the shine and this floor will disappear. Jill continued into the mall promenade, where shops were being shuttered, great gates being drawn across their entrances. Death-knell for one more evening.

She said goodbye to Alex and Claire and began the closing-up tasks. This consisted of locking the cabinet where the checkbook stayed; locking the cash register, and lowering shades on display windows. Alex and Claire had placed dust covers over the racks. These routines were acts of love.

Jill now thought forward to her simple meal, generally frozen quick foods that required nothing more than micro-waving. Used to her life alone; she had been sure she was complete. She thought about the day's chatter between her sales staff. Alex was to pick up pizza to take to his wife and son. Claire would hurriedly stop by the cleaners for that special dinner dress for her date tonight. Claire had nervously explained that she expected big news this evening. Her steady, now returning from a trip, had called to say—maybe they should look more seriously at their future together.

While Jill compared the lives of Alex and Claire to her own solitary life, she took the beautiful child mannequin, Tommy, out of his central spot in the main front display window, then she left the store locking the door behind her. Her purse hung on one shoulder and the mannequin, Tommy, was thrust under her arm. Actually, she had choice, she reminded herself as she walked to the car. Examining her circumstances, as she often did, she thought— there is always Robert. Older and divorced, he was charming dinner company, but driven to fill each hour of his life with such daily maneuvers as racing into the city to attend a gallery opening, then off to the club for a frenetic tennis match, then over to the studio for ballroom dancing. One could easily become exhausted just listening as he proudly announced his schedule. Too frenetic, too driven to be taken seriously. He didn't appear to exist if minutes and hours were left unfilled. And there was the time he took a woman he did not know at all, had not met before, with him to Paris for Christmas week. He couldn't tell Jill enough how uncomfortable he had been—stuck with that yapping, silly woman for an entire week. Up until then Jill had given him more sense.

And there is Jack, married and complaining, whining even, that his wife was a pig and he was on the brink of walking out. The brink however, never seemed to arrive, and Jill, seeing it all clearly—did some of her own whining—correctly established who was really the pig. Told him she was very busy these days.

With Tommy standing on the rear floor of the car, Jill wedged through tight traffic toward her expanded cape, bought after her mother died; the over-big house of her childhood. That was also when she bought the children's clothing store.

And there is always Clifford, she continued the review of her situation, with his hot tub under the stars. An interesting man, Jill liked having dinner with him—listening to classical music, hearing about his travels. But there was always his too evident eagerness too soon; "Why not jump in the hot tub. Why not stay overnight." Too many women, Jill knew, had done their turn in this same hot tub. Better to keep him as a light, not too frequent, dinner companion. They could practice their culinary talents on each other.

At home, Jill put away a few packages, and taking care with each placemat, napkin, and silver, she set the table for two. Then opening and heating a can of beans, she microwaved a chop and filled her plate, placing it on the table opposite the other chair where Tommy stood before his placemat. She ate slowly as she gazed at the mannequin's large, fetching, child's eyes, and tiny cherub face. It was hard to take her eyes off his face. She imagined what it would be like if he could move, even run, or reply if she spoke to him. His warm smile held Jill's fascination long after her plate was empty.

It was not that she wasn't active, her walls were lined with her paintings and awards, and there were painting workshops to attend, and competitions to enter. But in those quite moments, finishing up the day's chores, Jill had to pause to understand that . . . *Ours is not to see what lies dimly at a distance, but to do what lies clearly at hand.*

Finally, she cleaned the dishes, washing and setting them in the rack to dry. Then, standing the mannequin, Tommy, by the door from which she would leave in the morning, and smoothing out his clothing, she pictured how she would open the shop early in the morning and have him back in the display window before Alex and Claire arrived. In fact, she had done so many times before.

# The Brat

They waited at baggage claim for their bags to come round on the conveyor, and while they waited, the brat, Aggie, launched determined kicks at Claire's legs. While Claire quietly danced a sidestep, trying to avoid Aggie's constant attacks, Keith pretended not to notice. Or perhaps he really didn't notice. Tall and handsome in his Chesterfield coat, he kept his gaze fixed on the baggage conveyor. Claire, acting as though nothing unusual was happening, winced and shook with each violent kick from the five-year-old child. Maybe she could stand one more kick. And then one more. Maybe for Keith there was no limit to how many kicks she could stand.

Standers-by watched—some wishing they could intervene, but soon bags came, and, relieved of that responsibility, people found their bags and hurried out.

As she did at the start of each day, the receptionist wiped off the polished mahogany front desk. While she did that, the computer whiz watched and scanned the plush reception area as she relaxed in a side chair. It was early and the other employees at Keith Wadrow Promotions hadn't yet arrived.

"So Keith has found another sucker," the whiz said to the receptionist.

"Yup. He's acting more content these days, and he's getting personal calls now and then from a certain woman."

"Anyone I'd know?"

"No, this one's an unknown . . . Claire somebody. Apparently, she's Keith's neighbor in Greenwich. They met there. His looks and power, and his money, will always catch another one. Little do they know."

"Was that court case ever settled?"

"Yes. He's free once again. No woman can stand to live with the brat, and he never disciplines that child. Doesn't recognize her serious personality problem. I'd say the child has Borderline Personality Disorder. Makes you wonder what's in store for her . . . and him, when she's a teenager."

"She's over the border all right . . . clinically psychotic, my guess," said the whiz. "Man, do I hate to see Keith coming in with her. The last time the brat was here, I was out to lunch, and she crawled under my desk and unplugged everything, server, modem, everything. I had a time of it getting everything back online."

"Tell me about it!" the receptionist said. "That was the time she thought it was so funny to throw my jelly beans around the office. And I had to pick them up. Keith thought that was okay . . . just part of my job. He scarcely noticed and said nothing to her. If he brings that child in again and leaves her with us, I think I'll write a new job description and ask for a raise. A big one."

"Fat chance. You know our pay is terrific. And

the contacts . . . you love working here for the contacts. I know I do. I love seeing the stars that come in. And Keith knows that. He knows he could get a hundred women in a heartbeat to replace us. And we've met a few thrilling dates here, to boot. And many memorable parties to attend."

"Well, we're lucky for the most part that, except for occasional office visits, unlike his girlfriends, we've been able to avoid his child.

"That child's a bad seed. Too bad we can't warn his latest . . . Claire . . . you said her name was. Once when Keith brought Dinah, his prior, in with that child, the brat snatched my scissors and tried to jab Dinah. I grabbed the scissors . . . Keith saw what was happening, but said nothing. I wonder how long it will take Claire to drop him."

"If she's at all normal, she will soon. Maybe the benefits of going out with him are still too attractive. As usual, with those benefits in the offing, it takes a little time."

While she waited for Keith, Claire turned to see her profile and adjust her hat. Hats were coming back in style, and with an elegant hat tilted down over one eye, one could look mysterious, interesting. Not too big a hat—people shouldn't stare at the hat—just at her. Her lean straight body, and chiseled face, attracted her share of glances. Keith would be pleased—he loved to be with such a woman. Claire knew that. Although he was certainly cold, she was working on warming him up. He excited her, made her churn with anticipation. It was worth putting up with his strange child. But what to do about the child? Keith didn't recognize the seriousness of Aggie's hostile and aggressive acting out. He had said her behavior was just temporary acting out from having a famous star for a mother, one who was never home, and who didn't give the child attention when she *was* home. He had to compensate for that, he had said, so he often took the child around with him, convinced that in time that would heal her.

But that wasn't the only kind of attention the child needed, Claire thought: she needed strict limits for a few years, some that she could learn to trust; along with a hearty dose of psychiatric voodoo.

Well, she didn't want to lose Keith. He took her to famous places where there were famous people. She was living!—the quiet little Claire from Tulsa. Going to hot places at locations mentioned only on a website, and only if you had the code, could you access the information. With him, the ride was wild—he was always networking, watching for a new star; one not too messed up yet. And lovely little trips; they had just returned from a first-class weekend in Hawaii. There, Claire had hoped that showing Aggie how to build sandcastles would quiet the child for an hour or so, help Aggie to like her more: accept her in Keith's life. Instead, for three days, Aggie had screamed, "I hate you." Even on the plane coming home, Aggie had kept up the I-hate-you shouting, until the flight attendants and passengers focused stares of amazement at them.

Before she got to the door, Claire heard the child's scream, "I hate these flowers!" She opened the door and there was Keith holding in one hand a bouquet, and in the other, the child, her mouth wide-open howling. Keith, holding the flowers above his head, was trying to stop Aggie from plucking the blossoms. Petals lay about their feet.

Claire tried to speak over the child's screams. "Oh, I thought we were going out to dinner. Sorry, if I misunderstood."

"We are," Keith said. "I can't seem to get a sitter anymore, and anyway the child needs parent time, and restaurant training. I hope the formality at '21' subdues her. Roger, the manager, is a good friend; he understands."

While the driver waited with the limousine, Keith kept an iron grip on Aggie's gyrating body, as they stood just outside the door. Claire quickly attended to the flowers, her hopes for a romantic evening with Keith, seem to wash down the drain as she filled a vase with water and arranged the bouquet. The petals of one stem lay outside on the stoop where Aggie, with her desperate little hands, had managed to pull at them.

When Claire came out, Keith helped Aggie into the car first, then Claire; afterward taking his seat by Claire.

"I have to sit in the middle," Aggie yowled.

"All right," Keith said. He opened the door and got out. "Everyone out," he ordered. "Claire, please take a seat by the door. Then, Aggie you get in next." After they were settled, he climbed in, sitting next to Aggie.

Claire said nothing while they completed this arrangement—just followed orders.

"You can't sit next to my daddy," Aggie shouted, glaring up at Claire and jabbing her finger into Claire's thigh. Keith accepted this, his face immobile, his thoughts appeared to be flung far off. On the drive down to Manhattan, Aggie alternated between jabbing Claire's thigh and snapping her finger on the back of the chauffeur's head.

"I'd love to eat upstairs," Claire said, as they entered the restaurant. "I've never been up there."

"My Dear, that would be nice. However, with Aggie . . . the bar lounge is a better choice, noisier. And the ceiling toys will help distract her. Upstairs is as quiet as a tomb."

"I hate a quiet room," Aggie yelled. She lunged her shoe at the maître d's console. "I want to eat in the lounge. I have to see the toys!"

When they were seated, Keith handed Aggie an iPad® he had brought along to help keep her occupied while they ate. He had long ago learned that the quiet use of pencil and paper would hold her attention exactly one minute, and then be flung on the floor.

Claire studied the menu, but her thoughts were on Keith. Why couldn't he have found a sitter for Aggie? She ventured a tentative and risky hint, "Do you have reliable childcare?"

Keith appeared not to hear as he surveyed the room, nodding to acquaintances.

"Dear," Claire said a bit louder, "Do you ever use a sitter for Aggie?"

"No! I hate sitters!" Aggie insisted.

Keith turned to focus on Claire's face. An exquisite face, good bones, good to be seen with. "I gave up on sitters. They're busy all the time. I've tried to keep an au pair, but they just don't know how to handle Aggie. She's a little diva. Divas want what they want, when they want it."

The music, that by now Aggie had found on the iPad®, was asserting itself loudly, as Aggie, now standing in the aisle, gyrated about, waving the tablet over her head. Keith rose and snatched her back into her seat. He stopped the music. Then he showed Aggie a game app that he hoped would distract her from starting the music again. That seemed to work long enough for him to turn his attention back to Claire.

"There are a few connections I can bribe into staying with Aggie, but she raises a fuss if I don't take her everywhere with me now. And it's good for her to have a broadened experience before she starts school."

"I'm never going to school. I'm going everywhere with Keith," said Aggie. She had both hands on the tablet, shaking it violently. "I want the music!" she wailed.

"It needs a rest for a minute, Aggie, then perhaps it will play again later," Keith said.

He continued answering Claire's question. "She started kindergarten recently, but Porter's said she needed another year of maturing at home. They said she needs more of her mother's care, but you can imagine how that would be, with her mother off around the world making one movie after another. Shannon's career, as you know, is spectacular, thanks to me. I promoted her career, but not . . . her mothering instincts." He gave Claire an ironic smile as he popped an olive into his mouth. Satisfied with that answer, Keith eyes swept the room again. Several people raised a wave.

Aggie seemed to be taken with the idea that the tablet had to rest. For a moment she was quiet while her suspicious eyes circled from Keith to the waiter, who was now standing at attention by their table, and back to the tablet. She listened to Keith and Claire ordering, her narrowed eyes on guard for any devious plots.

"I want peanut butter and jelly," she ordered, "and sugar cubes. I want sugar cubes. NOW!"

Keith said to the waiter, "Peanut butter and jelly for Aggie, please. And . . .," he drew a deep sigh, "sugar cubes."

Now there was a lot of commotion as a famous couple entered—one whose careers Keith had managed.

"Ah . . . there're Julia and Brad."

Before the couple had a chance to be seated, Keith waved them over to say hello, and to introduce Claire and Aggie. Aggie sat still long enough to study the couple, then she carefully selected an olive and flung it at Julia's white silk dress. As though nothing important had happened, not even stopping mid-sentence, Keith reached over and move the dish of olives across the table.

"I want those olives," yelled Aggie, her voice loud and penetrating.

Fortified with his engaging smile, Keith steered the couple over to their table and briefly chatted while Julia dabbed at the spot left by the olive.

"I'm so sorry, Julia, you know how kids are," Keith said. "And with her mother gone all the time, I'm afraid it falls on me to be Aggie's full-time parent."

With spectacular incomes from movie careers that Keith had guided, Julia and Brad could supply a small nation with silk dresses. Julia managed a gracious smile. "It's nothing," she said. "There's no need to apologize."

Aggie, meanwhile, had found the delights of kicking Claire under the table. After the third kick, Claire moved her chair around the table opposite Aggie; far enough that Aggie's foot couldn't reach.

"Well, that was nice," Keith said, as he sat down. "I recently pulled together a new movie contract for Julia. You'll be seeing her in *Dare to Dodge* before long." He appeared not to notice that Claire had moved around the table.

With dinners before them now, Keith and Claire had a sense that, while Aggie was busy taking apart her peanut butter and jelly sandwich, they should utilize the lull and eat fast.

Soon, when Aggie's interest waned for dismantling the sandwich, Keith started the game of identifying toys and icons jammed overhead on the ceiling. In the past, this had kept Aggie's attention long enough for Keith to eat. But Aggie's spirit had been rising in response to Claire's moving across from her to where her foot couldn't reach, and she stood, marched around behind Claire's chair, jerked Clair's hat off, tossed it on the floor, and proceeded to vigorously rock her chair. Before Claire had time to set down her wine glass, it shook, sprinkling wine down her arm.

Waiters standing toward the back, unobtrusively shook their heads, looked at each other. One hurried over, handed Claire her hat, and with his towel, dried her arm. Was there anything else he could do? he asked. Before Keith or Claire could answer, Aggie, bored with bothering Claire, was shaking someone else's chair. The stranger stood up, looked around to see who was responsible for this awful child, and focused on Keith. Without apology, Keith rose and yanked Aggie to the back of the room.

"Would you kindly give Aggie a tour around the kitchen?" he asked a waiter. Normally, Keith didn't ask—he told. He was used to demanding and getting what he wanted. However, he knew these waiters were on duty and really had no time for tours. Even so, the waiter took Aggie by the hand and disappeared with her toward the kitchen.

Claire took a deep breath. Perhaps the peace would last through desert and coffee, she hoped. Please, twenty minutes to let her nerves relax. She wanted to enjoy her time with Keith. He was a beautiful man; she wanted to caress his face.

Keith ate in silence while continuing to look around. There were people here whom he had helped, people who had helped him. People who took quick glances at Claire, as though asking themselves whether she was someone they should know.

But their peace was short-lived: Claire despaired to see the waiter approaching with Aggie in hand. Gripping both Aggies' arms, the waiter dragged and pulled her along, as she used her loudest siren in protest.

"Sir, we can't keep her sweet little hands out of the food, and the stoves, are very hot. I thought it best if I brought her out of the kitchen before she got hurt. And, sir," he whispered quietly, "when I stopped her, she bit me."

"I understand," Keith said. "Kids will be kids, you know. We have to leave now anyway. Thank you for trying." He pulled from his inner jacket pocket a bundle of twenty-dollar bills that he discretely placed into the waiter's hand.

As soon as the waiter released Aggie, she threw herself on the floor, kicking and wailing. "I wanna go back in the kitchen!" She grabbed the waiter's ankle and hung on.

Trying to concentrate on their dinners, the nearby patrons averted their eyes and struggled to keep their conversations going. Though the lounge was a rather noisy place to eat, nothing could equal Aggie's disturbance. Waiters attempted to hide the confusion, kept busy with this and that, more than necessary; '21' felt a shift in the universe.

"We have to go now, Aggie," Keith said. He pried her fingers off the waiter's ankle. "It's getting late and we still have the drive up to Greenwich."

"I don't care! I wanna see the kitchen again."

Struggling to hold her arching body, Keith picked her up and followed Claire to the exit.

On the drive home, Claire and Keith could finally sit back and relax.

But not right away.

First, Aggie amused herself by tapping the chauffeur on the back of his head. Then she stuck the tablet, now blasting out reggae, up to his ears, and shouted, "Do you know this?" At last, she slumped down on Keith's shoulder and fell asleep.

For the rest of the ride to Greenwich, no one said a word.

He felt the lashes again. Even now, thirty-five years later, Keith wondered how his mother could have allowed her most recent husband to abuse a small boy. She didn't know about the kick across the room, or the back-handed slaps; for those, she could be forgiven. But she knew about, and condoned the beatings. The kick across the room had been especially devious. His stepfather, with a rare smile for Keith, had waved a finger and beckoned him over. Keith expected a treat or at least something good. Maybe this man had taken a turn, actually liked him—wouldn't slap him. Keith went over to him.

"Now turn around," the stepfather had said—again with a smile and with a sweet expression he rarely used.

But when Keith turned around, the man planted his foot in the middle of his back, and gave a shove that sailed Keith across the room. He just managed to catch himself before he hit the opposite wall.

"Now pick that up!" His stepfather spoke—his face wild.

What had he left where it shouldn't have been? Keith could no longer remember, but he had had so few possessions, it couldn't have been much more than a coloring book. He had not been able to defend himself. He had had no voice.

Each shout from Aggie was a shout at that stepfather. With each kick Aggie hurled, Keith felt a little revenge. Maybe if she could kick enough people, he could beat his stepfather.

# Bubba's Sidewalk Café

Directly on the sidewalk concrete slab, lay bacon sizzling in its own fat. This fat gently slid down from the bacon to the next slab on Bubba's left, where he now broke a dozen eggs to fry. Knees nearly up to his chin, sitting on his little, but solid, wooden platform mounted on rollers, Bubba rolled along from concrete slab to slab. With the slant of the sidewalk just right, fat from the bacon would finally reach the end slab where Bubba, satisfied that they were crisping up nicely, would turn thinly sliced potatoes.

For two seasons of the year, the sidewalks of Birmingham, Alabama could run up to one-hundred and twenty degrees Fahrenheit, and Bubba's short-order meals cooked slowly, but they yielded that subtle flavor that comes only from ground-level tender coaxing along in the boundless outdoors.

On the upside of the slabs, next to the bacon, simmered a pot of grits in which from time to time Bubba would give a gentle stir. And next to that,

95

slices of robust bread were slowly turning into toast. On the upside of the toast simmered a large pot of hot coffee, which from her home across the street, Mrs. Eva Lynn Savage carried over each day.

Bubba's sidewalk Café was on North Twelfth Street and his Twelfth Street neighbors lined up for their breakfast. Mostly an older neighborhood, they shuffled along, were not in a hurry. They came with plates, forks, and cups, and lined up one behind the other, enjoying the good hot weather. Whites, blacks, veterans from various wars, draft dodgers, spinsters, undertakers, plumbers, writers, children and pets, all chatting amicably, waiting, plates in hand.

The breakfast was free, but the Twelfth Streeters brought the food for Bubba to cook. He received no pay, but his own food was generously provided. He was more or less looked after by the Twelfth Street residents. Now, after giving the toast a turn, Bubba rolled down the sidewalk, stirring grits again, flipping bacon then eggs then potatoes, and finally, sizing up things, would call out, "Ready."

Bubba's Sidewalk Café had not started out as such a big venture. It all began after a string of powerful thunderstorms had lumbered through taking with them all power lines. Then Bubba appeared—homeless, nameless, and scared—and no one, including himself, knew from where he had come. It was as though his life had begun on that day. In fact when asked, that was the only answer he could give.

The people of Twelfth Street sat on Preacher Savage's front porch at night discussing Bubba. Not knowing what to call him, they just referred to him as Bubba, a good old southern nameless name. Preacher Savage and his wife, Mrs. Eva Lynn Savage, offered to let him sleep out back where their back porch had a tiny room just big enough for one single bed piled with pillows, sheets and blankets as needed.

In time, someone sitting on Preacher Savage's front porch asked whether Bubba shouldn't be in school. So they took Bubba around to several schools to test where he would fit. At Martin School, Miss Wilhite asked Bubba to do the multiplication tables. But when Bubba asked whether he was to do them in hexadecimal or binary, Miss Wilhite asked what did he mean, and Bubba demonstrated both. She then asked where Bubba had learned that way to do math, and Bubba said he didn't know; he just knew it. Another teacher asked Bubba whether he knew how many days in a year, and Bubba asked—for which planet? They asked Bubba to write an essay about the stars and he asked most politely which galaxy had they in mind? and in which language? Except for his origin, there seemed to be nothing for which Bubba had no answer. The good people of Twelfth Street and the teachers shook their heads and jostled their eyes about.

"I'm happy as I am," Bubba assured them. "I know enough to fodder my dreams. And the good people of Twelfth Street love my sidewalk cuisine. Couldn't I go on cooking for you?"

The Twelfth Streeters allowed as how that was what they really wanted, and so no more energy was expended toward educating Bubba. Besides there was no teacher who knew what Bubba was talking about. Which galaxy? Wasn't there only one? The Milky Way?

But back to Bubba's arrival: the day he arrived, Bubba was so hungry that he knocked on a door and asked Mrs. Florence Lee for an egg. Temperatures were just right for that egg to cook on the sidewalk. Bubba knew—for it would cook his feet if he stood there too long. While his egg was frying, the Twelfth Street residents came out to see what Bubba was doing huddled over the sidewalk, and saw his excellent way with that egg. And soon, Mr. Smith, who had missed breakfast because he had to go downstairs to open his mom-and-pop grocery store, at a time when Mrs. Smith was off visiting her daughter in Phoenix City, asked Bubba to cook an egg for him. And he brought one out from his store. After watching those eggs cook, the Twelfth Street people went inside and came out with bacon. Try this, Bubba, they said.

And so Bubba's menu grew, each thing tried in turn and proven tasty. People watched, then brought out more eggs and china plates and silver forks and knives and little Windsor chairs on which to sit up behind the café, up on the shady lawn of the Fountain Heights Weather Bureau, and talk while they watched and waited. Dogs and cats came, but kept quiet at a respectful distance as any well-bred southerner would do. And, for the animals' patience, they were rewarded with tasty, wholesome scraps.

Soon electric power was restored to Twelfth Street, but Bubba's Sidewalk Café was popular and congenial, and his deftness with his slabs and with flipping his spatula was too successful for the residents to ever stay in and do their own cooking. The people of Twelfth Street found it easier to eat at Bubba's Sidewalk Café; saved them the trouble of cooking indoors in hot kitchens. All they had to do was buy the food, and wash their dishes. Over time, spatulas and other cooking utensils were donated to Bubba's café, and in order to save his knees, Deacon Brown had fashioned the roller platform, altogether making Bubba's operation quite efficient. Other than his own personal plate and fork, the only inventory for which he was responsible was a few spatulas, which, after washing with baking soda that Miss Susie donated, he hung on a hook in the little back room. When the Twelfth Street denizens had eaten all they could, Bubba would scrape down the six concrete slabs with water and vinegar that Preacher Savage brought out in a large pail.

At this time, Bubba was about twelve, and he could not think how he came to be so. He had no memory of having had a home or parents. And anyway, it wasn't in his nature to wonder about such things; he took one day at a time. He couldn't remember any warmth except that of the sidewalk, and now that of the amiable Twelfth Street residents, always happy to line up to eat.

And so it went.

On Sundays, Preacher Savage arrived early to counsel his flock, and would walk up and down before the line of hungry people and give each person, dog, and cat a blessing. And Brother McCain brought out hymnals that he passed down the line. And while waiting for just the right turn of the eggs, those good people struck up a chorus of *On a Hill Far Away Stood an Old Rugged Cross*—most appropriate for Twelfth Street as it was on a slight hill, thus facilitating the rolling of bacon fat onto the slabs where eggs and potatoes lay sautéing. And, while Mrs. Cornelia McDaniel held her place in line, Miss Susie directed the singing by pumping her arms about in awkward arcs. Meanwhile, Brother Ray and Mr. Mack had pushed the piano in the prayer-meeting room of the Fountain Heights Methodist church up to the window so Brother Ted could play for the choir. Due to parallax, the choir was always one measure behind Brother Ted. However, no one seemed to notice, too stunned by the consistently high-pitched chirruping chords Mrs. Thelma produced. Then once breakfast was finished, the residents would stroll up the shady lawn toward the Weather Bureau and compete at horseshoes with shoes that had recently been removed from Nellie, who grazed at Preacher Savage's watermelon farm out in Roebuck.

Afterward, Mrs. Eva Lynn Savage took the grits pot in and Mrs. Sally Jones took in the coffee pails, and each customer took in his or her own plate and utensils to clean. Chairs were left in place ready for dinner.

Bubba—after his slabs were sparkling clean, boiled in the sterile heat—would shoot marbles with some of the local boys until the sun had passed over the tower on the old Weather Bureau; which event was a signal to begin cooking dinner with chicken and corn and green beans and okra that people were dropping by. The sidewalk retained its heat well into the night. And the Twelfth Streeters would gather in the listening dusk, sipping their iced teas and talking about little Princess Ann and little Prince Charles, and wondering about the nature of things: that some people were white, and some people were black, and some people were princesses, and some people were princes, and some people were not.

Then at night, Bubba would shower off with Mr. Greeley's hose and go to his little bed. Or, if during winter months the little back room struck him as perhaps too cool, he might slide down Preacher Savage's coal chute and warm himself by the stoked-down, but still hot, giant octopus furnace.

In winter, the sidewalk café had to close and the Twelfth Streeters would practice cooking again in their homes. By now Bubba was so entrenched in the hearts of the Twelfth Streeters that they would move him from house to house and cook for him, while telling him to eat up, stay strong, for the time to reopen his sidewalk café was but around the corner, but a month into the future.

The Fountain Heights Methodist Church stood next

door to the Weather Bureau. Lost to memory was the location of the eponymous fountain, but that didn't dull fervor, for on Wednesday evenings, after the sidewalk café was cleaned, prayer meetings were held with much joyful singing; Brother Ted Watkins worked the piano. Brother Ted's fingers were all over that keyboard and he hadn't missed a note in forty years; a compelling feat considering he hadn't seen a note in fifty years, nor had he seen anything else in all those years. He was sufficiently filled with a spirit that guided his hands over the ivories, and in a quick hurry, if needed. Actually, it wasn't fully known whether he missed notes since the boisterous voices would have drowned out an occasional sour chord.

The church's monthly potluck suppers, followed by checkers competitions, had always been held in the great hall in the Fountain Heights Methodist Church, but now, it was getting to where no one wanted to rise up to the cooking, their being dependent on Bubba. Thus it was proposed that Bubba try coming in on potluck night and cooking supper using the Fountain Heights Methodist Church's gas stove. Though Bubba's sidewalk methods were now solidly fixed, he agreed to make this winter accommodation for his good patrons. So it was, that once a month for potluck suppers—which weren't really potluck since Bubba planned and cooked them on the gas stove—Bubba moved indoors and fed the Fountain Heights Methodist Church congregation. Something was missing, though—everyone agreed—though delicious, it was not the same as Bubba's Sidewalk Café; did not at all have the same quality. There was something about the sidewalk that imparted its own characteristics, like aging wine or beer in oak.

Fame for Bubba's Sidewalk Café grew until Mr. Ray Ryan, a Birmingham News reporter, stopped around in search of a news item. Once he learned that all he had to do to eat at Bubba's Sidewalk Café was to bring a plate and fork and a few eggs or chicken—as the time of day required—he then became a regular, and wrote many rave cuisine reviews in the newspaper about the café, and published photos of Bubba, resting on his rolling platform, raised spatula in hand about to flip an over-easy. And from the newspaper article, people from the surrounding streets got a whiff of events on Twelfth Street; they had anyway wondered why the aroma of bacon cooking, wafting over to those notable streets, was so pervasive. They started coming round and soon, Preacher Savage and Deacon Brown had to wash off three more slabs for additional bacon and eggs and potatoes.

Now the line was longer with the addition of neighbors from Eleventh and Thirteenth Streets, some of whom, not understanding Twelfth Street culture, tended to be pushy, and caused Twelfth Street denizens to establish a patrolman (free meals, bring a plate and fork). Constable Ephraim would walk back and forth in his snappy uniform, which sight subdued any noisemakers. After all, the Weather Bureau official had to listen to the wind, if there was wind; rather efficient he was in leaning out the window to hear and feel the velocity and direction. Yes, he could stick out his finger, but to be more accurate, he needed his ears and finger.

Soon Bubba's Sidewalk Café was inadequate to handle the lengthening lines of hungry patrons. Nevertheless, Bubba didn't want to turn anyone away and thus he included more slabs and put in more hours. The sidewalk café soon occupied all the concrete slabs from one corner to the other. However, due to its nature, customers could line up at certain central points in the middle, as well as at the ends.

Work as fast as he could, it was hard to keep up, and Bubba hated to see hungry people having to wait; he had to take on helpers. So he brought in his marble playing pals to help. The marble players, used to crouching as it were, were natural cooks for Bubba's Sidewalk Café. Deacon Brown hammered up several more rolling platforms. No remuneration was provided, but meals were included, for the Twelfth Streeters supplied extra groceries.

Even with the additional work, Bubba was happy as long as he could continue cooking and eating his two meals a day in his accustomed manner. His sidewalk was sacrosanct; it was the way by which he had come to his expertise. Moving up in the world was for Bubba moving up the sidewalk. He had begun to think of Twelfth Street as home, and its residents as family. Now, in this heat of popularity, dishes rattled up and down Twelfth Street, and traffic had to be closed off such that Miss Susie and Mrs. Patricia Smythe erected stalls to display and sell their crochets and quilts. Reservations became a requirement, and now rules had to be posted: Bring food, plates, forks and cups. If you want to sit, bring a chair. To further ensure order, a friendly patrol of watchful pets was instated, and although in general people were waiting calmly, some of the cats who attended ballet school at Miss Nancy Lum's, would practice their tours en l'air and jetés to provide entertainment during the wait.

Time came when the City of Birmingham demanded that the crowds stop messing up the Weather Bureau's lawn. Grass was turning to dust, and after all, that Grand Palazzo style building was a showcase. More meetings were held on Preacher Savage's front porch and forceful letters were written to the Birmingham News editor until finally, the city was brought to its knees. A city official who had dined at Bubba's Sidewalk Café, and who had seen its value, and who had passed by an open window of the Fountain Heights Methodist Church, and who had heard Brother Ted's fingers on the piano keys, and who had heard the choir and the voice of Mrs. Thelma—which reminded him of his grandmother's warbling—thought of a way to appease the city. The next week a van rolled up outside the café and unloaded, right down the middle of the closed-off street, many, many little iron tables and chairs, thus saving the lawn.

Eventually a Taxing Authority thought he saw a loophole he could plug, and came sniffing round to assess, but the Twelfth Street residents rose up and pointed out that the sidewalk café had no income, and no money changed hands. Still, the Taxman said, there must be value-added-value of value to the city, and for finding which, he would be rewarded.

No.

Bubba didn't even accept tips. And everything was cleaned up and off the street by dark. Besides, someone pointed out, Bubba provided a gratis service to the town: when the Weatherman needed to know the temperature, he would call out his office window to Bubba, who would tell him how fast or how slow the eggs were frying. Of course in winter the Weatherman had to work harder; put out a pail of water to see whether it accrued ice.

Well, at least the city could tax Bubba for the use of the sidewalks.

No.

The Twelfth Street residents owned and maintained their sidewalks.

While these discussions were taking place, Mrs. Eva Lynn Savage slipped inside and returned with a plate, fork, and cup, for Bubba to hand the Tax

Official a plate of eggs and bacon, along with soul-fortifying coffee. Eventually the Taxman saw their point, and, becoming a regular, dropped his case.

The success of Bubba's Sidewalk Café allowed Bubba to franchise his café which provided additional employment for Birmingham residents, especially for marble gamesters with their particular crouching talents. And the City Fathers, to show their appreciation, raised funds for a Dali designed, tessellated statue of Bubba. To this day, it sits in front of City Hall, made of the original six slabs, covered with fake meals in progress, backed up by Bubba, knees nearly up to his chin, spatula at the ready, sitting on his roller platform. In order to honor Bubba in this prime location, the city removed its statue of "Stonewall" Jackson.

This is the etiology of sidewalk cafés.

# An Algebra Problem

With calculating glances, Maria looked across her living room to where Peter and I sat. Believing that two positives multiplied together would result in a greater positive, Peter and I had just married— suddenly as it were—and this was my first introduction to Maria, Peter's mother. She acted—well—not pleased, and seemed to struggle to remain neutral; what else could she do? She had no words of welcome or affection for me, or for that matter for Peter: an indication that our equation might become a challenge that I hadn't counted on.

Peter and I had dated for only three months before we married, but we had observed and had known each other longer than that. *Known* isn't really the right word; it would be more correct to say we had frequently met at church functions.

Peter's long, slim hands and his silky black hair combined with his tall slender frame to form an exponential power that touched me right off. And I liked his manner when he spoke before our group.

But prior to three months back, we had not said more than two words to each other.

One evening after a church program, Peter asked me to go for coffee, and as we sipped coffee in Starbuck's lounge, everything seemed funny; we laughed a lot. Peter's being eleven years younger than I was seemed to be a positive rather than a negative—subtracted nothing from our potential. Rather, in a strange way, my extra eleven years added something—maturity, he later said. He seemed to be quite relaxed with me, and I was growing warm and cozy feelings about him.

I loved his flat abdomen. He said he liked to look at my interesting and pretty face. Both of us tall and slender, we seemed to fit well together.

Three months later, when he asked me to marry him, said he wanted to be married to me more than anything, and (I laughed to myself), he had cooked for me and had told me that I had pretty feet: you gotta marry a guy who can cook, and who thinks your feet are pretty, right? I saw us as two binomials forming a perfect quadratic. I did love him, and I said yes.

Within three days, we had obtained a marriage license, found a Justice of the Peace, and married. For a while, it seemed insignificant that during the marriage ceremony, the JOP droned on and on until I could no longer hear what he said. Perhaps that was why I soon feared that this marriage equation had some equalities. What had the JOP promised for us?

Afterward, Peter and I still lived in two different homes—Peter rented his, I owned mine free-and-clear—two binomials to be solved. And I had a cat: figure in Tom cat; more about him later.

* * *

"Toby was due an hour ago," said Maria. "He called

to say he was driving over from Spokane. I hope nothing has happened to him."

Although he made no comment, Peter's face fell, seemed to drop into sadness. Toby was his son from a long-ago marriage and they had not kept in touch. I sensed that, although Peter didn't believe what his mother had said, some hidden meaning, some impulse of hers affected Peter negatively. Slouching, he grimly tried to disappear into the overstuffed, chintz, paisley chair. I learned later that Toby *never* drove over to Spokane. Could it be that Maria was inventing a situation: purposely inventing an uncomfortable situation for Peter? In fact, the bulk of Maria's conversation was to check her watch and say, "I wonder where Toby is? I hope he hasn't had an accident."

I pushed aside the feeling that the direction of our daily lives might already be sloping into negative territory, since a negative (Maria)—times two positives (Peter and me)—still equals a negative. And even a negative mother is yet bound to be a required part of the equation.

With each of Maria's statements, Peter would draw a slightly concerned, but bored, look and would either say nothing, or would grunt, "Huh."

I admit I was unable to calculate an outcome for this strange puzzle, or to think of a factor to add that would balance.

Non-specific chatter continued, with Maria's never speaking directly to me, or even looking my way. I keenly felt the zero by which she multiplied my presence. I needed no refresher to remember that zero, times any quantity, is zero, and I felt null, indeed.

Suddenly, for no apparent reason—Peter had been all easy compliance, saying nothing challenging at all—Maria verbally attacked him; embarrassed both of us with an outburst, "Don't you think you're something, Petey boy!"

Peter gave no response. Attempting to let his eyes focus on nothing, he slouched further into the chair.

"You think you're really something, don't you!" she continued, intensifying the challenge.

He looked a little sadder, and continued to give no response. Was she referring to this new marriage? The pretty new wife? Did Maria want to keep this equation off balance? Did she plan to cancel it before it counted for something?

With pretend hugs and cheek-kisses around, we soon said good-bye and left for the elevator. Shutting Maria's apartment door behind us, Peter and I breathed easier; relieved to have finally escaped this barking mad, or in any case, strange, woman who seemed bent on unbalancing our trinomial.

"She's always like that," Peter said as he pushed the button to bring up the elevator. He couldn't lift the sad look from his face. Before I could think of an appropriate but kind reply, we heard Maria's door open and shut, saw her coming toward us.

Peter's eyes rolled, "Oh, no," he said. He had had enough for this day.

"I'm going to see you down." Maria grinned a silly pasted grin, as now she seemed calculated to appear friendly; although still no word, gesture, or glance for me, still the zero. The elevator ride down was silent, but I thought Maria's grin loudly mischievous. At the ground floor, Peter and I were further relieved that Maria found acquaintances with whom to chat, and allowed us to go on our way.

\* \* \*

Except for one other group of diners, the Russian restaurant where Peter and I were treating Maria to lunch, was empty. Although she knew her way around Spokane and was still driving about, every two minutes, Maria asked, "Where is this restaurant?" and Peter or I would once again patiently tell her the location—right on Main. This kept up until Maria took a long scheming look at the pretty blond waitress.

"Look at her, Peter. Isn't she beautiful!" Every two minutes Maria prodded Peter in this manner. "Peter, see how beautiful she is!"

The first time I heard this I politely agreed; although I wished my new mother-in-law wouldn't point out other women to my husband. His reaction was slowly to sink into his chair, while trying to look as noncommittal as possible. Did I feel more sympathy for me, or for him? The waitress—petite woman with silky hair the color of pale citrine—was indeed easy on the eyes. Pretty. When she came over to our table and anchored herself next to Peter's chair, Maria exclaimed:

"You're such a beauty!"

With limited English, struggling with a thick Russian accent, the beauty seemed more than pleased to open up to us. Maria would roll her eyes from the beauty to Peter. With his eyes on a position under the tablecloth, he seemed to wish to roll into a ball under the table. And I wanted to give him a push. Both he and I were mute as this play unrolled before us. Even after she had brought our meal, the beauty held her ground next to Peter, and while we ate, Maria continued to chat with her.

As we were now the only diners, the beauty was free to hold forth with us, and she appeared to thrive on Maria's attention. She remained riveted close to Peter and gamely entered into this two-way conversation with Maria as though she were part of our party. From across the table and over the aroma of our lunch, I could smell the beauty's perfume. And, as I look back in my mind's eye I think I see that her hand was on the back of Peter's chair. It was taking me a while to learn that this was a typical female response to him: magnetized by his lean frame, nice face and black hair like silk—women were easily caught in his gravity.

"What is your name? Where are you from?" Maria asked. The beauty named some town in Russia, and since Maria's ancestors were from Albania, I observed that this information increased Maria's enthusiasm by a power of three; for me, a negative power of three. I could see the minus sign hovering in the air over our entrees, floating on wafts of perfume, subtracting from my goodwill. With each reply, Maria would eagerly nod to Peter; that knowing *see what you're missing* look rigidly fixed to her face.

I couldn't enjoy the meal, and sat silently wishing I could eat in peace, not be forced to attend to this exclusive interchange. Peter's dejected face wore the same wish. Maria continued, alert and lively: dementia had taken a pass it seemed.

"Where do you live?" she asked the waitress. "How long have you been in the U.S.?"

In her halting, few words of English, the waitress said that she hadn't been in the U.S. long, a few months. This was evident, I thought, for her scant words of English hardly added up to two sentences; I could do the math in my head. She was going to school, she added; which additional information, for some unknown reason, caused Maria to issue another encouraging glance to Peter. To give him credit, trying hard to ignore them, he looked anywhere but at his mother or at the beauty.

Obvious to me, and I hoped to Peter, although I had no way of knowing, was that on no occasion had Maria said a word to me. She had shown no interest in me, not to even acknowledge that I was there. She had managed, through skills unmatched in my experience, to factor me out of the equation. One form of a quadratic equation equals zero, and I had become the zero.

Now, finished with our meal of long endurance with the beauty never moving from beside Peter, I hoped Peter would say let's have our check so we can get going. But his mother and the waitress continued their act, and I watched Peter, who appeared to be in agony, wait it out. Finally, tired to my zeroed bones of this thirty-minute, two-way, and now rude conversation, and thinking that there would be no end, I stood and announced, "I'm going to the lady's room." Perhaps this would somehow alter events, adjust this—for me—negative formula.

But when I emerged from the restroom, woefully I saw that Maria and the waitress were still engaged in lively discourse; the beauty looking as though she didn't intend to move. Ever.

I think that Peter had continued to refrain from joining their conversation. However, Maria had pulled from the waitress all personal data, including that she was unmarried, and where she lived. With each bit, Maria would look to Peter, as though she were handing him important information that he was expected to use.

I had giving up on wishing that other customers would come in to unglue the beauty from Peter's side, and I could no longer sit at the table and feel like a victim to this, and so I said, "I want to get some air. I'll be waiting out by the car," and I gathered my purse and jacket and walked out.

In the parking lot, without car keys, I stood leaning against Peter's car, until after ten or fifteen minutes, Maria and he came out of the restaurant. I had forced them out. I imagined that Peter, rousing to my displeasure, finally inconvenienced himself and

Maria enough to look up at the beauty and say, our check please, we must go. I imagined Maria writing down the beauty's phone number, or better, asking Peter to write it for her, and then with a pointed look, asking him to put it in his pocket. Peter would have done so to humor her. Any solution to my sense of well-being with these people resolved in imaginary numbers that I could not parse.

Later, weeks later, while going over the problems of this marriage, a friend told me that I might have challenged Maria before she started conversing with the waitress. Right after her first few urgings to Peter to admire the woman—I could have asked, "Aren't you happy with the wife Peter has? Are you piping for him?" My friend said this kind of challenge would often stop malicious intention in its tracks. I was soon to find out that I needed more of these smart challenges to Maria, but was never able to come in with one at the right moment.

Some days after this lunch, when Peter and I were on one of our six-mile walks, he told me that his mother had always been like that. She would take him, or his father through the hospital where, in days gone by, she had worked, and point out the beautiful women, enthusing as they went, "Isn't she beautiful!" Urging whoever was with her, husband or son, to stare at the woman. Peter said he had always thought that she pushed other women onto his father.

The day he told me this, I said, "Perhaps your mother is a latent lesbian."

"What?" he stared at me.

"Well, it's known that certain women get sexual gratification through a vicarious association when their husbands shag another woman."

"I can't believe you said that," he said.

But I let it hang, and subtracted a large coefficient from our equation.

* * *

Peter knew his mother liked Wendy's chili, and embarrassing though she was, he continued to try, together with me, to keep contact with her. This day, we were seated at Wendy's with Maria and Peter's sister, Inez. Peter had asked Inez to make the two-hour drive to Spokane to help him assess their mother's condition. As well, he wanted reinforcement for taking away Maria's car keys; she had been slipping more each day into dementia. Indeed, she had just been diagnosed with Alzheimer's, but Peter refused to use the term, seemed to refuse to acknowledge this power over his mother.

Maria, seated across from Peter and me, nodded toward Peter's ear and the half-karat diamond mounted there. "Did Peter buy you a diamond like the one he bought for himself?" she asked me, looking at my ring finger.

This may have been my first sentence from Maria, and I remember being quite taken by surprise. But I rallied with a positive, "No," and organizing my face into a look that said I'm so happy with our substantial gold bands, I continued, "We decided on gold bands," and as I fingered the band, I smiled at Maria as though I couldn't possibly have wanted a diamond; absurd thought.

Maria nodded knowingly. Later, a friend suggested that I should have said, "Oh, yes he did, but it's so large that I don't always wear it." Clearly, anyone who was still warm would have thought that if Peter had bought such a diamond for me, I would be wearing it, proudly displaying it third finger, left hand where the more modest, but determined gold band rested. And I pushed down the knowledge that only ten-months' lease payments on Peter's Escalade would have equaled quite a few karats.

\* \* \*

When it came to deciding where Peter and I would live together—he did not want to move into my un-mortgaged house with its tiny, old-fashioned bathroom and small kitchen, nor did I want to move with my cat, Tom, into Peter's rented house, where—Peter insisted—Tom would have to live in the cellar (with standing water). Tom would claw Peter's very special speakers (Peter predicted). Had the cellar been Cat-Paradise, I still would not have dispatched Tom there. So, putting aside for the time being the problem of Tom, we began to look at real estate, hoping to find our ideal home together. Despite Tom, Maria, and house issues, we did enjoy our marriage. During these early days, for the most part, as I had Tom to take care of, I stayed in my home, Peter stayed in his—nine miles from me, although we were often at each other's house.

\* \* \*

"I'm taking mom for lunch at Applebee's. We're just leaving the clinic now. Can you have lunch with us?" Peter asked over the phone. Maria's condition was deteriorating, and adding to the mix, she had just received a diagnosis of pancreatic cancer. Her days were numbered, but I refused to even think about adding those numbers to my calculations.

"I'd love to," I replied.

"Good, I'll pick you up in fifteen-minutes."

I hung up the phone and proceeded to freshen my makeup.

Maria now had begun to lean daily on Peter, tightening her grip. Her calls—three and four a day—were for him to pick up her prescriptions, find her lost medications (someone was stealing them, she said), find her lost tax documents, find out when were her appointments, take her to appointments. On  one occasion I watched Peter ignore the insistently ringing phone. Without moving, he listened to her voice message drone on. Exasperated with her mixed-up, confusing demands, he did still feel his obligation, such that he no longer had time to house hunt, or to think about moving, much less hang out with me. With his putting in almost daily care for Maria in one way or another, he and I had difficulty keeping in touch; I could almost hear terms falling from our equation.

Of course Peter's always being on call to help Maria was admirable, but her needs seemed to be fictitious, contrived; she seemed to use her illness to benefit her schemes. Still, we had to grant her the benefit of doubt, so on this day I was happy for the invitation to join them for lunch, happy that he wanted to include me, happy that Peter and I were carrying on with our marriage—such as it was. Perhaps we could make it.

In fifteen minutes, my phone rang again. It was Peter. "I'm sorry that I won't be picking you up. Mother doesn't want you to go. She says she's not dressed for company." He said it exactly like that.

"Oh, that's alright," I replied. "I understand." I did not understand at all, but what else could I say? Apparently Maria was dressed well enough for Applebee's.

* * *

We drifted on in this haphazard manner, and then one evening when Peter picked me up for a dinner out, he said, "We have to stop by mother's apartment just for a minute—she called to ask me to. I'll be only a minute."

In Maria's apartment building, on each floor, before the bank of elevators, was a small cozy lounge with tables and overstuffed chairs. And as we stepped out of the elevator into the lounge on her floor, I said, "Your mother probably wants to talk to you alone, so

I'll wait for you here." For other than the diamond question, Maria had yet to converse with me about anything. I took a seat in the lounge and Peter unlocked and went into her apartment. I always have something to read, or to write, and made myself comfortable with something of that nature. But within five minutes Peter came back out to me, rather in a panic.

"I don't know what to do," he said. "Mother has packed everything she owns and says she's waiting for the movers to move her to the lake. I mean *she has packed everything*, and she is determined. Won't listen to me. I've argued with her that we are not going to the lake, but she is adamant. I don't know what to do. She can't even go to bed, for her sheets and linens are packed. Can you help?"

Calling on me to help a woman who appeared to hate me, hate my existence, called me to question how much help I could be; however, Peter clearly was feeling panic, needing assistance of some sort, from somewhere.

"Don't argue with her while she's intractable," was my first idea. "Humor her."

"You try," he said. "Come on." And he held her door open for me and followed me into the apartment.

We found Maria sitting on her bare bed, while all around her bedroom were boxes, waste cans, and suitcases stuffed with her packings. One box held her carefully folded bed linens. Showing in another were cosmetics, hairbrushes, shampoo, and such that ease a woman through her day.

"We're going to the lake," she said. "The movers will be here any minute." Then she asked me, "Are you coming too?"

I was surprised that she looked me square in the eyes and spoke to me directly. I was thinking—your son and I are married—it's not likely that he will leave me behind. Still, considering her dementia, I said yes, reluctant to begin the lies that I knew had to follow; what would we do if they didn't work? I forged ahead with a really smart fabrication and said, "The movers called to say they couldn't make it tonight, and will be here tomorrow." Miraculously, Maria believed me, though I had to say it several times. I don't think Peter could muster the courage, still he did try to agree with me, reinforce my statements. But it was up to me. In my defense, I thought that by the morrow, Maria would have forgotten about moving, and would instead be wondering who had rearranged and packed her stuff. I count this as the only successful formula I was able to devise that entire year.

After repeated urgings that the movers would be along tomorrow, Peter said it was bedtime and we would make her bed, which we did; although it was late now and the energy for making a bed seemed beyond my remaining supply. Maria accepted this outcome, acknowledged that she would be going nowhere tonight, that she was to go to bed. This equation was unsolved, though—for one, we were unable to find a mattress cover, and the thin sheet looked inadequate, barely hid the printed mattress beneath, and we were leaving with packed containers strewn about the room. Yet I was thankful to have it done, and to be able to leave. Maria allowed us to leave. I left wondering how she would find anything in the morning, wondering how, living alone, did she managed to maneuver through her days. Peter said he could move her to an assisted-living apartment in the same building, but the expense would be more than hers or his finances would support.

I heard no more about moving to the lake; somehow it had resolved itself.

# An Algebra Problem

\* \* \*

Now, Peter, slowly coming apart, started a program of counseling with his best friend and former employer, a man who claimed to have a Master's degree in counseling, but had never worked in the profession. Strange ideas evolved from these counseling sessions, one of which was Peter's sending me off to buy colored tee-shirts for him. He was to wear only gay colors, bright colors, happy colors, yellows, oranges, reds. He asked me to find and buy these for him; he just didn't have the time. He said he couldn't be sad while wearing bright colors.

\* \* \*

"How're you doing?" Peter said to me over the phone. "Sis and I went to the Trattoria for lunch," he continued—sounding happy to be giving me good news.

Inez had come to town again to spend a few days helping with Maria, and she and Peter did finally find and take away Maria's car keys, and very soon in fact, sold the car. Now daily Peter would call me to say that Inez and he were running around together doing this and doing that; had lunch here; had lunch there. While they had solved previous problems; had worked out a formula for having fun, I felt increasingly like a zero: I was never included. And, as well, from his tone, they were not helping his mother much, nor were they sad about her illness, but were having a rollicking good time. Trying to graph the sense of it all, the direction of these parabolas, I saw that Peter and his sister's association was on an upward trajectory, while his and mine was slanted down. Nothing computed to my benefit.

With or without colorful, cheerful shirts, Peter's self-control diminished in lock-step with his mother's

119

further deterioration. Sitting in church with me one morning he wept inconsolably, shoulders shaking. For now Inez had returned to her home, and these days Peter was happy and light-hearted only when talking and laughing with Sharon.

Sharon had arrived with Robert: two experienced caregivers hired to alternate with Maria's care. Engaged to be married, they were usually at the apartment working together around the clock. On the one occasion when I had been invited to join them, Sharon and Peter sat in Maria's front room chatting about trivia, laughing as though Peter's mother was not in her bedroom engaged in dying. When I said that I should be able to be of some help, Peter suggested that I stop by McDonald's and bring meals for the three of them. Up to now, I had more than felt left out, and so was eager to do this. Didn't complain when no one offered to reimburse me. Robert ate his meal while he sat beside Maria's bed, listening to her breathe. I sat with Peter and Sharon while they ate. Unable to wedge into their animated conversation about growing up in Spokane, I soon left.

Maria had calculated that she would not run out of money before she ran out of life, and in the end left eleven thousand dollars for Inez and Peter to share. I watched Peter's excitement grow by a power of two, as, like a little boy, he rushed out to buy spinners for his leased Escalade. Toys. I said nothing but I thought he might better have paid down some of the debt he had acquired buying motorcycles.

Try as I might, I was still unable to balance this equation: I wouldn't move into Peter's rented house, putting Tom in the cellar; Peter wouldn't move into my house with its small, old-fashioned bathroom. Moreover, Inez was back, and while cleaning out Maria's apartment, she and Peter were running around having lunches together again, never inviting me to join. He would call me in the evening to regale me with these stories. Although I would sometimes find myself searching, there were fewer and fewer pluses to offset the minuses.

Although Maria's negative presence was now subtracted from the equation (which actually was a positive), the foregoing, together with my growing fear that I could become responsible for Peter's increasing debts, activated my desire to be out of this unfulfilling and imaginary marriage. And so one evening, after hearing more about several lunches with his sister, I said:

"If this is how it's going to be, we might as well get a divorce."

Peter agreed; he wasn't surprised. During this time, while growing away from me, he had been growing proportionately closer to his sister; clearly this ratio did not work in my favor.

"I know how to file for our divorce," he said. "I simply pick up the forms and together we fill them out. Then I file them with the Court, and unless we cancel our application within ninety days—we will be divorced. It's as simple as that."

Indeed, in the end, simplifying and balancing our equation couldn't have been easier. On an evening, rather sad, but inevitable, we sat together in my home and filled out the forms. With no children together, no mutual debt, nothing owing to one another, all we had to do was sign, sign, sign. Peter filed our forms with the Court, and in ninety days we were divorced. Our marriage had lasted ten months.

\* \* \*

But it turned out that that was not the end. The quadratic equation of our lives continued to entwine each of our binomials. Now that Maria's apartment was finished, now that Inez had gone back to her home, Peter, feeling lost without all the distractions,

121

continued to ask me to join him for this and that. A divorce does not keep two people apart—especially two people who still cared for each other on some level, and have not yet established other options.

"I want us to marry again," Peter said to Dr. Evans, the marriage counselor we now faced across his consulting room.

Peter seemed to have satisfied his need to grieve by spending numerous hours at his mother's grave, and now he wanted to see whether we could resurrect something of our connection. Although for the past three months we had spent little time together—what with the illness, the confusion, and the death—he still needed me in his life, that was now emptier than ever. Putting aside the problem of Tom and speakers, we looked at a few houses, yet in our discussions we couldn't get passed a mortgage problem. Peter suggested marriage counselling and that's where we were this day.

"I think Peter should draw cash from his retirement for his half of our new home," I said. "After all, I have no mortgage and I don't want to acquire one. When I sell my house, I will be paying cash for my half of our new home."

"I'm not going to take money from my pension," Peter said to Evans. "I intend to finance my half."

"Is this a show-stopper?" Evans asked me.

"Yes. No mortgage."

"Then we're finished," said Evans. "You're through. There's nothing I can help you with."

"Okay," one of us said. Clearly we were being dismissed; we stood to leave, said goodbye to Dr. Evans and left. The suddenness of his dismissal: such as there's no equation that will apply to you two, left numbers twirling, jumbling in my mind. It was true; I couldn't put them together in any workable arrangement.

As we were leaving Peter said, "Care for a bite?" It was early and neither of us had had breakfast. As we faced each other across the table at Denny's, we agreed that this was indeed the end. Peter looked sad, and I was sad. Another ending. If you multiply two negatives together, you have a positive, but I could find nothing positive in this outcome, except that I was stalwart about not taking on a mortgage. Why? Because down the road Peter could pull out leaving me with a mortgage that I could not afford. He had pulled out of two other marriages, had a habit of financing up to the max anything to which he took a fancy, and though he had a good income, in my mind, he had become a financial risk. He had recently bought a second motorcycle, joking that he would have to find a job to pay for it. I could almost see the negative powers of our equation increasing exponentially.

Whereas before, Maria had represented the "X" term, it was now Peter's role. As I felt more positive, he looked more negative, and a negative—times a positive—equals a negative. No matter how I calculated, we would lose, and I calculated that if we joined in marriage, I stood to lose the most.

Now, even though we recognized that this was our end, so to speak, Peter continued to ask me to have dinner with him, and I continued to yield. It was the kind of situation wherein one postpones the inevitable. Then one day the equation resolved itself without my help or interference. I heard that it happened this way:

Without a mother in his life, without a marriage companion in his home, without a way to pay his increasing debt, Peter's frustration and loneliness one night forced him out on a long-endurance motorcycle ride up the Palouse, until both he and the motorcycle ran out of gas. The next day he was found babbling incoherently, walking alongside the highway. Peter never regained capacity to make decisions.

Of course I was grieved, I had not ever wanted mischievous luck to befall him. During that last year, I visited him many times, but I could not now find anything about him that would add up; I could not change his exponent from a negative to a positive. Moreover, without the negatives from him and from his mother, I was surprised to find myself feeling quite positive for a change. I was able to move on and to resolve the equations of my life.

Peter had become the zero.

# C. L. I. K.  Man

Amber limped along with one shoe off and one shoe on. While struggling to manage her valise and umbrella, she clutched the broken shoe and stiletto heel to her chest. Perhaps it would be easier to take off the good shoe and walk up Fifth Avenue barefoot, or rather in her nylons, she thought, than to hobble in such an absurd manner. But the pavement was grimy with slush. Rain hadn't stopped the pelting it had released all afternoon, and she couldn't bear to dirty more than one foot. Alas, it wouldn't be easy now at 5:00 p.m. with throngs streaming out of doorways, headed home to peace, or maybe screaming kids, or maybe a stack of bills; anyway anxious as all get out to hail a cab. During her career as a psychologist, she had heard all the stories.

With one foot up and one foot down, she lined her thumb up with all the others and stretched out into the street for oncoming cabs, but a cab would hardly see her. Should she invoke her power? Perhaps just push a micron bit of it into her thumb?

But with chilly rain slanting into her face, when the stranger, who had just snared a cab, beckoned for her to share it, she swiftly closed her umbrella and, clutching her valise, umbrella, shoe, and heel, slid bottom first, into the cab, drawing in her wet legs, torn stocking, one foot in a stiletto heel, the other foot bare and dirty.

"Ah, you're a life saver." She took in the man's easy face, as he tried to help her manage her things.

They discussed their destinations—which one to give the cabby first. They both lived on the eastside around midtown. Convenient.

That settled, Easyface spoke: "I'm Brickly, and I'm pleased that I spotted you before we drove off. I saw you standing in that puddle with a bare foot and a broken shoe, and I just knew that you would be going in my direction." He was dressed like an artist, or like a caricature of an artist: beret, ascot, paint-smeared smock, and espadrilles—also paint-smeared. Yellow hair curled under his beret and dropped down around his neck.

Amber nodded her appreciation, and Brickly went on talking.

"Brickly is an ancient family name. I come from an ancient family. They're all ancient . . . mother, father, aunts . . . they're all as old as you can get and still be taking up surface space." He thought out loud. His skin yielded a distinct whiff of vodka.

Amber knew that odor.

He hadn't allowed Amber to say her name. "I've just come from badgering my trustee into releasing more of my funds," he said. "The expense of supplies is breaking me."

Too much information. Amber didn't want to hear Brickly's woes. Going over her own finances for the past few hours meant giving her adviser free analysis—just part of being a psychologist. With that, and the blowing rain and broken shoe, her energy was temporarily drained. She nodded.

"As you may be able to tell, for I notice perceptive intelligence in your face, I'm an artist," Brickly said.

Amber smiled in recognition of the reds and greens cavorting around his smock, and, she noticed, under his fingernails. Still he had not given her a chance to speak, nor did he seem to care. Probably not interested. Still, his face was nice. Also, his smile.

He positioned himself sideways, better to see her. She wasn't comfortable under his gaze, and focused her attention through the window toward the sidewalk at wet reflections and umbrellas moving, jostling.

In the bumper-to-bumper commuter traffic, the cab barely advanced at times. Commuter stress flared outside the cab, but Amber and Brickly were dry and headed in the right direction.

"I like what I see," Brickly said.

Amber gave him a quick sideways glance, then leveled a hard stare at him. "That's enough . . . if you don't mind. Sharing a cab with you, accepting your courtesy, does not equate with your getting personal, or invasive. And, for the record, I'm only interested in C.L.I.K. men."

"Excuuuuse me. Maybe you would allow me to show you that I'm a true gentleman . . . a true believer of women as delicate flowers, to be enshrined in glass cases." He thought for two seconds, "and, what kind of man is a click man?"

Amber rolled her eyes in a manner that said let's get this cab ride over. Maybe she should ask the cabby to stop now and let her out. "I'm a psychologist, and in my practice, I've developed a theory to help the frustrated women I counsel: if they focus on accepting only the attentions of a CLIK man, they'll have fewer relationship ups and downs to endure. So far, I find you fulfill only one-quarter of the equation."

"Really. How is that?"

"You seen to be kind . . . that fulfills the 'K' . . . 'K' for 'kind.' "

For a few seconds they listened to the horn music of Manhattan. Bright red taillights blinked up Fifth Avenue as far as they could see. The cabby caught a glimpse of his passengers in the rear view mirror. Up until now, he'd overheard every possible conversation.

"Click. How do you spell that?" Brickly asked.

"C. L. I. K."

"Right . . . I've met a woman who can't spell."

"Take my professional word for it . . . it's my theory and it's spelled C. L. I. K."

"And the C. L. I.?"

Amber didn't reply.

Undeterred, he launched on; he had interesting information to impart, "You should see what I'm painting now. Really. Stop by. You know those wonderful old murals in the RKO building? Well, they're so damaged by air pollution that they've been carefully removed for restoration. I'm painting new murals in their place. Come and look." He had still not asked her name.

She challenged him: "You spoke of needing more funds for supplies. If you are paid to paint murals then you already have that cost covered."

"Ah . . . perceptive lass. Quite true. Let's just say I need the funds for other ventures."

"Your vodka supply running low?"

"Ouch," He looked at her in mock surprise.

Except for the street's cacophony, they rode in silence for a moment.

"I know your neighborhood," he said. "Used to have a studio in a closet there before I became famous. Now the RKO building supplies a studio for me. Say . . . , there's a nice bar in the Hotel Plaza Athenee, you've probably been there. It's just a block or so from your street." He waited for affirmation, but Amber said nothing. "Let's get out there and have a bite to eat. Though I had nothing to do with breaking it, I want to make amends for your broken shoe. Then I want to find time to paint you. Maybe I'll put you in one of my murals."

How he does blather on, needs a taste of discipline. But, he could be blasphemed, Amber guessed, without a single dent to his shell. "You would have to clean up before I would be seen with you," Amber said. "Look at you . . . covered with paint and dirty fingernails."

The cab driver, fascinated, his eyes black and round as the tires, watched them in the rearview mirror.

"Well, mam, I can hardly wear gloves and paint, not with my technique which takes a lot of scraping. Sometimes I have to use my thumbnail. But the Athenee loves me. You'll see, they'll make a fuss over me . . . even when I'm paint-covered. I'm usually paint-covered. Come on I'll prove it to you." Without waiting for a reply from Amber, he instructed the cabby to stop at the Hotel Plaza Athenee.

Amber knew of the Athenee restaurant's fine reputation. It would be wonderful to relax there and listen to this nut. He was stranger than her usual clientele. And she was hungry, and it had been a trying day. If she went along she wouldn't have to think about cooking dinner.

When they arrived at Athenee, Brickly hopped out and in four steps made it around to Amber's door, opening it before she could gather her shoe, heel, valise and umbrella. He took her arm, and in one lunge, grabbed the valise and pulled Amber out of the cab.

The Athenee maître d' did make a fuss over Brickly. He looked over Amber, and then smiled at Brickly as though, once again Brickly had taken an award.

"Michael, I'd like you to meet Claire," Brickly said.

Amber shook hands with the maître d' while giving Brickly a look.

"Amber." She wedged in the word.

"As you can see Claire is barefoot, except for ruined stockings. She's one of my usual misfits. Claire, who thought I shouldn't come in here paint-covered and with dirty fingernails. But for this broken shoe she would appear normal. But then whomever have you seen me with who looked normal?"

"Claire?" Amber asked.

Brickly ignored her.

"I don't see paint, sir," Michael said.

Brickly looked down at his smock surprised to see that it was fresh as though it had just arrived from the Chinese laundry around the corner, and moreover, his old, tired espadrilles looked brand new.

"And your fingernails are clean and groomed," said Michael.

Brickly raised his fingers to examine, "Shit. How'd that happen?"

Amber, alias Claire, tried not to wear her knowing look, but there it was.

The maître d' showed them to a corner table set with exquisite china and crystal and tall candles, lighted and inviting. He pulled out a chair for Amber.

Brickly took a seat opposite Amber and said,

"Michael, we'll have a magnum of your best bubbly. We have much to celebrate."

After Michael stepped away, Amber said, "Don't you think you've had enough tonight?"

"No, mam. I want to celebrate meeting you, sharing a cab, and . . . my retrospective at the Whitney. It's there now. I must take you to see it. Are you married? Don't answer. I know you aren't. I also know that you don't have a lover, or if you do, I'll chase him out in no time. Or is it a she, or maybe it's both, one never knows these days." He gave Amber a smirk. "Shrinks are weird anyway; comes with the territory."

"Whoever he or she is, it's none of your business," she said.

"Right now, I have more important questions." He looked himself over. "Imagine this . . . I'm spotless. How can this be? How did the paint disappear? How did my nails clean themselves? I haven't had clean nails for a year."

"I don't know," Amber said. "But now, you fulfill the 'C' word . . . 'clean.' "

He looked as pleased as though it had been due to his own accomplishment. Amber admired his confidence. She loved his face as well. His face—one she thought she could look at across the table forever.

Michael arrived with champagne, and held the bottle at an angle for Brickly's appraisal.

"Excellent, Michael, a fine Bollinger. Yes, we'll have that.

"Claire, let me order for you. I know the choice dish for tonight, Crab Provençal. You will be pleased. Have you had it before?"

"You could order it for Claire, if she is here," Amber said, "but I'd like to look at the menu, if you don't mind. Perhaps we should have a third place set for Claire?"

131

"If your name is not Claire, it should be. Claire is my favorite name for a beautiful woman." His eyes caressed her face. He noted the long lashes, the up-turned nose, reddish hair clipped back on one side by a sterling silver comb. "My wife's name is Claire. My mistress's name is Claire, and my daughter's name is Claire and now your name is Claire. You know why my wife's name is Claire? Because when I met her, her name was Boudica. That's not a name an artist of my caliber can abide." He spoke with run-on sentences.

He tried to continue the conversation, find out more about Amber, what were her interests, where did she come from (no one in Manhattan is from Manhattan), but when he tried to form the words, he couldn't make his lips move. In some mysterious way they were frozen together. What is this? He kept trying.

Amber stared at him a blank look and sipped champagne. Although he tried to hide his malfunction, she saw his distress. His puzzled look amused her. "Stop calling me Claire. My name is Amber. And if you have a wife, a daughter, and mistress, why aren't you with one of them?"

He couldn't answer. He looked helpless. His mouth wouldn't obey his command to talk.

Amber looked around the candle lighted dining room. With fine champagne, her mood became euphoric. Everything was okay, terrific, even though this man, who called himself Brickly, was strange. And with a wife and mistress, he was not someone for whom she would pick up the phone. She studied him across the table—noticed again his fine face and golden curls. And his distress. Let him have another minute before she released him.

"Don't call me 'Claire' again."

Now, as quickly as the hindrance had come upon

him, Brickly could speak.

"I know, your name is Amber. A corny name at that. I knew an Amber down in Tennessee. A real baby. She raised pigs and squealed exactly as they did. You weren't thinking of raising pigs were you? Don't. Christ. Don't tell me you were about to raise pigs. I can hear them squeal and oink already. You'll have to corral them in the corner before I'll come to dinner. You're not a baby. You're a strong, beautiful woman who should change her name. What were you doing in the RKO Building?"

Their waiter, Nick, stood ready to take their order. "It's good to see you again, sir."

"Hello, Nick. I'm delighted to see you too. My lovely companion and I are celebrating our new relationship. I found her stranded in the rain with a broken shoe. I rescued her." Without asking Amber, Brickly said, "We'll both have Crab Provençal. Their crabs are flown in fresh daily from Maryland," he assured Amber.

"Indeed they are, madam," Nick said.

"You'll love them," Brickly said. "Amber, you must come to see my retrospective at the Whitney." He flipped from topic to topic. "I'll pick you up tomorrow. I know you have no appointments tomorrow. I'd love for you to see how I game collectors. I take something simple, such as the wonderful curved lights I find in your eyes, and streak them with drips across the canvas. Totally unplanned. Then I cross that with elegant lines from your eyebrows. Then I add something from the day . . . whatever is in the sky: raindrops, haze, sun, clouds, leaves, confetti, diamonds. Purely farce. The more farce the more my collectors love it, Claire."

Nick placed entrées before them, and with a slight bow he asked whether there would be anything else.

"No, Nick, that's all for now." Brickly started to

pick up his fork and found that he couldn't lift his arm. He didn't move. He thought it better to hide his entrapment.

Amber pretended not to notice. She picked up her fork and selected a piece of crab, smacking to show Brickly what he was missing. Soon she asked, "Is something the matter? Don't let this marvelous crab get cold."

"I want to savor the aromas for a second," he said. Now he found that he could not lift his hand, let alone his arm. And again, he could not speak.

She watched him. "If you call me Amber, things might go better for you. I am not Claire. I will never be Claire. Let's try this again. The crab's delicious. Thank you for ordering it for Claire. Amber will savor it for her."

Brickly found now that he could lift his hand and arm, and he could spear a section of crab with his fork. He began to eat in earnestness. This woman, Claire-Amber, clear as amber, was wonderful, as in full of wonder. A fine claret. Give him time; he would have things under control soon enough. He always did.

When their tab came, Amber insisted on paying for her dinner.

"I want to treat you," Brickly said. "Show you how pleased I am about our future together."

"You might be surprised, my friend, but thank you for trying. And thank you for a nice evening; the champagne and crab were the best I've had in two years. Maybe even five years. And the company wasn't all that bad, either. Peculiar . . . but not bad," Amber said.

They stood at the door to her brownstone, her keys ready to open the door.

"I'll pick you up tomorrow at ten sharp for your

tour through my retrospective. We'll beat the crowds. Then we'll have lunch in Whitney's garden."

"How do you know I can make it tomorrow?" Amber asked.

"I know. I know." He said goodnight and walked off.

"But you have my shoe," Amber called out.

"Leave the shoe to me. I'll have it repaired. This shoe will never break again."

I could have fixed it myself, Amber thought. Just too busy to put my mind to it.

At the Whitney, Amber was pleased to see that Brickly's paintings held the crowd's attention. At least she thought the paintings were his; he said they were. And as more people began to gather, some recognized him and raved. Raved? Why would they rave over this paint-splattered drivel? But there you are. People said such things as; "I can see what you were doing here." "I can see what you meant by this curve." "This drop carries so much meaning." "Your white spaces send chills through me." Brickly filled women's dreams. The women eyed Amber.

"You see, my dear," he looked into her eyes, into her brain, her thoughts, "you haven't been reading the right papers. I'm famous. Claire, you excite me. I want to make you my slave. Or, if you insist, I'll be yours." Again he couldn't move his lips. He looked at Amber helplessly. Alright, I get it now. I won't call you Claire again, he thought. And his mouth unlocked. He took her arm and clung to her. "You will be mine," he said.

Not likely. Amber silently formed the words for him to see as she watched the crowd pass before Brickly's paintings. A rope had been installed to keep the unruly people a decent distance from his priceless work. "Along with your wife, daughter, and mistress, and who knows maybe more . . . ?" she asked.

"Yes. What does it matter? I'll paint you. You'll have access to my studio. You can bring me wine while I paint. I will caress you in between my masterpieces. You'll be allowed to keep your office hours, but only on my schedule. When I have to be at home with my wife, or keeping my mistress happy, you'll be allowed to see your clients. I'm sure you can untangle their messes. And here, by the way is your shoe." He pulled it from his backpack. It was the same shoe, but now it was purple and laced with green stripes.

"My shoe," Amber said. "It doesn't match the other one!"

"It's better, my dear. You must wear the old one and this one together. I insist. You must live! Live! Be free of convention. Anyone can wear matching shoes, my dear. You're not anyone." He leaned into her ear. "I have an insatiable desire for you."

Amber looked at Brickly with half-lowered eyes, "My desire for you is quite satiable . . . surfeited already."

"Ah . . . Claire."

The crowd let out a collective gasp. He turned to see paint whirling into small circles on the canvas before them.

"Jesus," he said. "What in hell?"

"Poor boy," Amber said. "Things will go badly as long as you call me Claire."

He stared in disbelief as the guard called a curator to see what had happened.

While they dined over lunch, Amber finally realized that Brickly indeed had the weird moxie to make it in Manhattan. And behind his bravado was subtle, inviting charm. His swagger . . . too bad there wasn't an "S" in the C.L.I.K arrangement. If he insisted, she would allow him to do a small portrait. Nothing else. She figured it would be along the lines of Picasso's Girl with Red Beret: wouldn't be a likeness, but would be interesting. Then, other than taking in an occasional show of his, she would take care not to be taken in by him. He was appealing, but lining up with his wife and mistress just to hang around for the charm and the fame wasn't her style. She would wait for a CLIK man.

She answered the phone.

"My love," Brickly said. "See how you've captured me." He could at least think *Claire*. "Did you catch my picture in both the Times and the Voice? I'll save copies for you. You can show your clients what a famous person you hang with. I want you to cement me into your heart. Now this week, I'm taking Wednesday to start your portrait. I know you are free then."

"How can you be sure?"

"Shrinks never work on Wednesday. Seven a.m. I'll pick you up; take you to my studio. After I paint you, you'll be as famous as Gertrude Stein."

That figures: just as she suspected.

Brickly executed Amber's portrait, size 14" by 18", primarily in soft blues and greens, with flickers of amber. Typical of what Amber expected, was her nose—off to the right, both eyes to the left. Surrounding all was a halo of reddish hair. She looked like an angel who had died and been reconstituted by an architect who had let water ruin his plans.

"See, my dear, I've caught your true persona. Best portrait I've ever executed; all because you inspire me."

"It is lovely, Brickly. And all done with only two

sittings. Had I sat for you again, you might have remembered where my nose is."

"Amber! Any face can look like that . . . so ordinary. I wanted to depict the upturn God molded onto your nose, while simultaneously presenting those searching eyes. Brilliant! And do you see that one of your ears is a gold heart? I know you have a heart of gold, and so I depicted it. I suspect the 'I' word is 'intelligence.' You must see now how intelligent I am." He cocked his head back in a gesture of pride.

"I'll cede you that, but blustering about it will reduce a capital 'I' to lower case. So watch it."

"Yes, mam." He took a bow.

"How long will it take to dry? When can I have it?"

"Oh, you have to pay first. I'll take it out in . . . shall we say 'trade?' "

"Yes, I'll barter," said Amber. "I'll offer you one counseling session for it . . . you need it."

"Only one? I'm sicker than that." He stood back, one arm crossed against his waist, the other up to his chin. He stared hard at Amber. She continued to admire her portrait.

"And . . . it's going in my next show," he said. "The title is . . . surprise . . . 'Amber.' It's been a great strain on me not to title it 'Claire.' You'll be famous. What will clinch the deal though is a figure of you nude. I'll paint that next."

"That's about as likely as my ordering a lobotomy for you . . . though a lobotomy might be a good idea."

"Fussy. Fussy. You aren't open to how much fun we can have."

"As much fun as a bee in my bra."

"You hate me. So uncalled for. I'm a loving gentle man. Just ask my wife and mistress. I'll give you their numbers." He collapsed into himself. Deflated.

Amber felt a spot of pity rise up; under his bravura was the little boy.

"Now when can I be analyzed?" he asked."

"I don't think you'll survive analysis . . . three years, a minimum. Or better, I don't think I can survive three years analyzing you."

"Ah . . . three years on your couch. Sign me up."

"I don't use a couch."

"Then some of your precious drugs . . . ."

"No drugs. I don't practice biologic psychology."

"No? Then what do you do . . . touch me all over?" He fixed her with a salacious grin.

"No, silly. I'm a talk therapist. No touching."

"Ah . . . my bad luck. My bad luck. Tell me Amber, how can I be close to you?"

"You can't. I can be close only to a CLIK man."

"But, I gather that I have fulfilled all the requirements except for the 'L' word. You haven't told me how I lack the 'L'. . . . I'm up for 'lascivious.' "

"The 'L' word is 'loyalty. That's where you come up short."

" 'L' for loyalty . . . ." He had to ponder that. "Well, can't the 'L' represent 'love,' as in I'll always love you?"

She thought, but didn't say, no. She was unlikely to revise a working theory. She gave him a smile. "I'll see . . . keep me guessing. Allow me time to think about the 'L' word."

# About Shirley Mason

During a career as computer programmer analyst, Shirley Mason wrote and enhanced software systems for computer installations in Connecticut and New York. Through those years there wasn't adequate time to raise children, paint, and write. So to keep thinking about words and putting one here, and putting another there, she wrote limericks and short essays in stop-and-go traffic. Long hours and long commutes did not allow her to take writing seriously until the end of all that commuting. These days, she writes, and in between that, she paints, and in between that she is a silversmith. And don't forget her cat, Sophie, whose name is not Schrödinger, but she wishes it were. Please visit www.shirleymason.com (WIP). (slarsen22@aol.com)